LEE YURI (Gangwon, South Korea, 1990) began her literary career in 2020 through the Kyunghyang Shinmun New Year's Literary Contest. She has published two short story collections, *Broccoli Punch*, which was her fiction debut, *The World of All Things* (2023), as well as a linked novel collection, *Meet Me in a Good Place* (2023).

AMBER HYUN JUNG KIM is a freelance Korean-English conference interpreter and literary translator whose published translations include Park Min-gyu's *Pavane for a Dead Princess* and Eun Hee-kyung's *Nobody Checks the Time When They're Happy*. She lives in Seoul.

Lee Yuri

BROCCOLI PUNCH

TRANSLATED FROM THE KOREAN BY
AMBER HYUN JUNG KIM

HÉLOÏSE
PRESS

First published in English in Great Britain in 2025 by
Héloïse Press Ltd
Canterbury
www.heloisepress.com

First published in Korea by Moonji Publishing Co., Ltd.
Edition published in agreement with Casanovas & Lynch Literary Agency

Cover design by Laura Kloos
Edited by Kim Stoker

Text design and typesetting by Tetragon, London
Printed and bound in Great Britain by CPI Group (UK) Ltd, Croydon, CR0 4YY

This book is published with the support of the Literature Translation Institute of Korea (LTI Korea)

ISBN 978-1-7384594-3-8

EU GPSR Authorised Representative
LOGOS EUROPE, 9 rue Nicolas Poussin, 17000, LA ROCHELLE, France
e-mail: contact@logoseurope.eu

CONTENTS

RED FRUIT

Dad had insisted I scatter his ashes in a flowerpot, which was a ridiculous request to make about one's cremated remains. But since my dad was the kind of person who would make such absurd demands all the time, when he told me what to do with his ashes, I simply nodded and muttered, *Will do*, with the full weight of the request only dawning on me much later when I was sitting on the bus headed home with the small urn containing Dad's ashes on my lap. *Hold on. This doesn't make any sense.*

The bus was full of people heading home from the same crematorium, all of whom were either crying, had cried, or looked ready to burst into tears. Compared to them, I looked like I was headed to a picnic with a basket on my lap. *Perhaps it* would *be nice to go on a picnic*, I thought, given the pleasantly warm weather we were having. My thoughts wandered to the local park not far from my house, then to the sandwich shop in the park, then to the realization that I was hungry. I looked up the bus route, having decided to go farther than my intended stop and get off at the park. Just then, somebody behind me started sobbing loudly, ruining the mood and therefore my impromptu plans for the park.

Two seasons had passed by the time I rediscovered the urn deep inside one of the pantry shelves. Mistaking it for oat powder, I scooped up a spoonful and brought it to my nose for a whiff. I didn't know what the urn was doing inside a pantry meant for non-perishable foodstuffs so I closed the lid and moved it to the space over the kitchen sink, relieved that I hadn't eaten any of the ashes. But the space above the sink wasn't such a great place either, because each time I stood underneath the kitchen hood, smoking, the urn came into my line of sight and made me uncomfortable. One lazy morning, I was standing in front of the sink, staring at the urn, only then realizing that what I took to be an urn made of pure jade was in fact made of plastic that only looked like jade on the outside. Taking a long drag on my cigarette, I was reminded of my dad's silly request and thought that maybe I should just go ahead and do as the old man had asked. After all, it wasn't a difficult request.

Even in life, Dad would ask for silly favors which grew increasingly absurd after he became ill to the point that I suspected he was doing so only to make my life miserable. Out of nowhere, he'd insist I head to the West Sea to bring back small fresh-fried crabs for which he had a sudden craving. He demanded that I call the public TV network and ask why his favorite host was no longer hosting his favorite morning talk show. When he heard about a pub that was renovated to look like a Japanese traditional building, he insisted that I head over there in the middle of the night and set the place on fire. *And if I went and did that, who's going to take care of you? You can't even go to the bathroom by yourself!* I retorted, which prompted him to angrily turn his back to me and lie on his bed fuming for the entire day, only returning to his normal self in the evening. *What's the difference between red bell peppers and yellow bell peppers anyway?* he had asked casually. At that, I had stopped in the middle of doing the dishes and scrolled through my phone with soapy fingers. *Apparently, red bell peppers are good for osteoporosis and the yellow ones for high blood pressure?*

I wasn't always so indulgent with him. There were times I lost my temper. Once, he dug out a few crinkled bills from under his duvet and asked me to buy him ten goldfish. Not wanting to start a fight, I took the money and bought him the ten goldfish he asked for at two dollars a pop. When I brought him the fish, he asked me to wheel him into the bathroom where he stayed a long time. When I sneaked a peek inside, I saw that he had released the fish into a full tub and was taking turns placing them on the palm of his hand and stroking them. *Dad! Are you out of your mind?* I yelled. He turned around and gave me a somber look. *I wanted to see if it's true that goldfish suffer burns at the human touch.* I glared at him from the bathroom door. *Seriously, what is the matter with you?!*

Dad, for his part, was also not one to be easily reckoned with. Each time I got annoyed with him, he would whip out his secret weapon, one he had no qualms about using whenever he felt the need to. The weapon involved a summer day we'd spent at an indoor swimming pool when I was six years old. I was playing in a small wading pool that reached my knees while Dad was swimming in the deeper pool for grown-ups, when suddenly, bored with the kiddie pool, I decided to venture over to the adult pool, where I proceeded to slip and fall in. It was a weekday morning and Dad and I were the only swimmers there.

Even in my thirties, I can still remember every single detail about that incident, including the layers of caked dirt in the corners of the glass windows in the ceiling, the faint smell of chlorine, and the way the water seemed to seep into every pore of my body, numbing my blood and overwhelming my every sensation—the way I reached desperately for the ground, hoping that my toes would brush against the floor and give me back the familiar feeling of touching land. Every time I recalled the incident, I would have an out-of-body experience, gazing down upon my thrashing self like an outside observer to what was going on. The scene was so amazingly vivid that it was as if I were holding a snow globe up to my eyes, where inside an ugly little girl in a red polka-dot swimming cap lay slowly drowning.

But there was one scene from that incident that I can't recall: the one where my father rescued me. It also happened to be the only scene from the day that Dad seemed to remember. When he saw me floundering, he swam out to where I was and held me up. This was his secret weapon. Every time I got annoyed with him or refused to heed his demands, he brought up the incident, and of how, when he pulled me up, I'd wrapped my taut body around his neck and pushed his head down as I scrambled to stay above water and take in gulps of air. He ended this story with the somber refrain: *If it hadn't been for me, you'd have drowned that day.* To that, I shrugged and retorted that it wasn't such a big deal that he'd saved me. After all, he was my father. But for some reason, I felt my throat close up and my body tighten every time he trotted out the story, and I would find myself heading out to the convenience store late at night to grab the coconut water he asked for or dialing the number for the electric fan manufacturer to ask them why the wings of their fans only spun to the left.

Dad is now dead and gone, but I become filled with the same helpless sensation every time I see the urn perched gently on the shelf above the sink. Unlike my living breathing father, I had no issues ignoring his ashes, which is why I decided to move the urn to the balcony and ignore his last request, thinking to myself I would stop by the flower market the next time I happened to be in Yangjae-dong. It was only after breakfast the next day and after I'd put on my makeup that I realized he'd gotten to me again, as I found myself dozing off on a bus headed for the flower market.

That same day, I came home bearing a bag of soil and a skinny little tree. The soil was one thing but the sapling was a miserable sight to behold, with only a few leaves trembling from its meager branches. I had been pacing outside a small, unintimidating shop in the flower market when its overweight owner came out to ask me if I was looking for anything in particular, to which I muttered something unintelligible as I couldn't bring myself to tell him I was looking for the best plant to dump my late father's ashes in. Seeing my hesitation, the man offered me the pitiful sapling in a cheap plastic pot. It had a name which I promptly forgot. When the owner asked for five dollars, I quickly handed him the money and left.

Back home, I spread some newspaper on the living room floor and brought out the urn. I dumped its contents on the newspaper and, with a heated gimlet, bore some holes in the bottom of the urn for water to flow out, then placed the ashes back inside, mixed in with some of the soil I'd bought. There were only a few fistfuls of my late father's ashes that weren't even that finely ground. Several fragments of bones the size of fingernails were mixed in with the ashes. While horrified at the thought of touching them, I became seized with a morbid curiosity to see them rolling around on the floor. I grabbed the biggest bone fragment I could find and held it up to the light, letting it roll while I imagined which part of my dad it came from. It was evening by the time I finished mixing the soil and powdered bones back inside the urn, or what was now a pot that contained the puny little tree. After generously watering the plant, I tipped the pot slightly to allow some of the excess water to seep out.

By the time I finished washing my hands in hot water, I was filled with an exhaustion so deep that I went to bed early. I had already forgotten about the plant by the time I woke up the next morning and didn't think to check on it. Unbeknownst to me, the wretched little plant grew and grew, sprouting tender green shoots and growing thick new stems. One day, as I was folding laundry in the living room, Dad spoke from the balcony.

"Water."

Stunned, I sat there for a good minute in complete shock. Then, muttering to myself, *This is just as annoying as when he was alive*, I went and filled a glass half full of water and poured it into the pot. Dad curled his leaves in pleasure as he drank.

Dad kept growing to the point where he needed to be twice moved to newer, bigger flowerpots, and now required more than one full cup of water daily. His leaves grew fuller and his branches thicker. Now a handsome tree, I suggested pruning some of the thinner brown leaves a little but his screaming and whining left me with no choice but to let him continue to grow wild all over the place. I sometimes regretted buying such a big plant and thought it might have been better to opt for a small pretty seedling, but at least Dad was in a good mood. Besides, all he needed was a little water and sunlight, so this made him much less high maintenance than when he was human.

Even so, Dad being Dad, he would ask for the weirdest things sometimes. For instance, he requested that I place him in front of the television so that he could "watch" a show on Korean traditional food all day long (although I wasn't sure if he was only listening to the show since I had no idea how he could see). He asked that I dig up one of his roots because he swore there were bugs crawling around underneath. When I waved him off because I didn't want to get dirt under my fingernails, he brought up the swimming pool incident again. "You know, back when I was still human, we went to a pool together, you in your polka-dot swimming cap..."

"Fine, fine already," I sighed and put on a pair of plastic gloves to dig Dad up and inspect his roots, which, of course, were clean and not infested with insects.

I work as a freelance translator of French novels and essays, which means that I work from home all day, although there are long stretches when I have no work at all. A recent assignment was to translate a French novel titled *Apple* by an unknown author, which was about a French woman who believed she was an apple. Ever since becoming capable of independent thought, the woman believed she was an apple. Instead of walking, she rolls around; instead of putting on makeup, she scrubs what she imagines to be her red peel to a sparkling sheen; for food, she only drinks water. One day, she sees a street vendor selling fresh-squeezed fruit juice, a sight so terrifying that she faints on the spot. When she comes to, she realizes that the fall she suffered when she lost consciousness was of sufficient strength to have split her down the middle with each of her halves lying sprawled on two hospital beds. Humiliated at having to display her insides and seeds for all to see, the woman plunges into deep emotional distress. In the split second that it took for her body to be cut in half, her mind seemed to also have been split down the middle, and it was unclear whether her intentions, her consciousness, and her willpower were in the left half or in the right half of her body.

Despite her doctor's best efforts, the woman slowly begins to rot away and succumbs to death on her hospital bed(s). Summoning her last bit of strength, she murmurs something to her attending physician who can't make out what she says. The woman's last words were a series of letters of the alphabet nonsensically strung together. Believing those utterances to have been the language of apples, the doctor grieves her passing. Having translated the novel up to that point, I couldn't help but smile at the idea of an apple language. After all, I had a father who was now a tree who has no trouble asking me to open the window or go fetch him a Coke.

In any case, *Apple* is one example of the kind of bizarre translation assignments I would receive and which I approached with no sense of urgency, although I was also known to throw myself into my work when I wanted to. While I worked, Dad would sit on top of the washing machine and bask in the glow of the sun, and when the sun's angle shifted, he would shout, "Yu-jin! Seo Yu-jin!" At that, I'd place my French–Korean dictionary face down in the shape of a teepee and head to the balcony to place him back in the sun, after which Dad would sit in peace again and I would go back to work.

Given that I no longer had to nurse my sick father, I had more free time on my hands, which I invested in my work, so that I was making more money than I had in the past. On pay day, I treated myself to a pretty little dress or some *galbi* beef short ribs that I'd marinate at home. I felt a little guilty about not including my dad so I started buying those plant food concentrates sold at gardening stores, the ones in small squeeze bottles. Dad claimed that the plant food made him feel young again. I couldn't tell whether he was talking about his days as a human boy or as a plant seed, and the more I thought about it, the confusion became so great as to threaten to split me down the middle, forcing me to stop. Just like that, Dad and I enjoyed those lazy days together.

A new year dawned. My short bob grew down to my shoulders, and my dad grew from being as small as a harmonica to the size of a violin. I had become completely adjusted to living with Dad the Plant by that point, and Dad had become equally used to living as a tree. I admit that we still had our arguments sometimes, and I sometimes felt the urge to chop him down, but for the most part we got along.

As he grew in size, Dad became bored with being confined to the balcony. At first, he asked that I open the windows so he could feel the breeze and look down upon the scenery. He delighted in seeing the crows and pigeons and the stinkbugs clawing up the window screen but he soon grew tired of those, too. One bright spring day, he bellowed, "Yu-jin! Let's go outside! I want to go outside!" I asked him if he wanted me to uproot him from the pot but he insisted on wanting to go outside the apartment. I tried heaving the pot up to my chest. It wasn't so heavy that I couldn't lift it but neither was it light enough to carry around.

"Sorry, Dad, I don't think I can do this," I groaned as I put the pot down again. His leaves sagged in disappointment.

When it seemed he had gotten over it, I went back to vacuuming the apartment and did the laundry as well. I was hanging my clothes out to dry on the balcony when my father spoke again.

"You remember when you were six years old? When you were close to drowning and you grabbed on to me and pushed me under so you could..."

The next day, I went to the local home supplies store and bought a wheeled hand cart. "Cart" might be too fancy a word for the dolly I bought, which consisted of a crude plastic box, a set of wheels, and a handle. But when Dad saw me walk in with the dolly, he was so excited his leaves shook with joy. I placed him on the cart and pushed him outside much like I would a baby in a stroller. It wasn't easy maneuvering the cart on the bumpy paths but it wasn't impossible.

"Let's go to the park. No, the bus stop! I want to go to the movies!" shouted Dad, his leaves practically dancing in excitement. Anxious that someone might overhear him, I muttered at him to quiet down. If someone had indeed heard us, they might call the authorities about a talking plant, and we would be swarmed by investigative journalists with their camera crews or the intelligence agency or even people from NASA.

I pushed the dolly to the park, then to the bus station, just as Dad had asked, where we sat and saw people getting on and off the various buses. Then we went to the movie theater and checked out the movies on the roster. On our way home, we took a shortcut through the park again. This route was to become fixed as our go-to route for all future walks. Once every two days, or at least once every three, I placed Dad on the little pushcart and took him on a walk on the same route. Sometimes, we stopped for groceries on the way home which I placed on the cart as well. Sometimes, we got caught in sudden rain showers that left me soaked and Dad's leaves green and sparkling like tiny little emeralds.

One day, we arrived at the park where I saw a man sitting on our usual bench and eating a sandwich. I lifted my dad and placed him on the bench next to me. Rubbing my knees, I sat down and thought, *I should also pick up a few sandwiches on the way home*, when suddenly, Dad whispered, "Yu-jin, look over there! Look!"

I looked up and saw that the stranger had a potted plant perched next to him too, about the same size as my dad's. The plant looked obviously well-taken care of with plump, healthy-looking leaves. Dad and I stole glances at the handsome tree, but the man kept on eating his sandwich seemingly without a care. When he was done, he crumpled up the plastic wrapper and threw it at a nearby trash can. The crumpled-up plastic wad traced a clean and lovely arc right into the dead center of the trash can. It struck me how silly it was to describe someone's act of throwing away rubbish as clean and lovely, and then a soft smile came to my lips. The man bent down and grabbed something from underneath the bench, which appeared to be a folded green pushcart in the same model and make as mine. The man pulled open the cart and placed his potted plant on it, then proceeded to push it down the beaten path out of the park. Dad and I stared at him as he tottered away, and we sat there in silence for quite some time before getting up and going home without stopping by the bus stop or the movie theater.

Two days later, we saw the man again. He was sitting on the same bench and eating the same sandwich, and after he was done, he crumpled up the wrapper again and tossed it at the trash can. This time, he missed. Looking embarrassed, he got up and headed over to pick up the trash, and for some reason this made me happy.

Dad was distracted by the man's potted plant. He couldn't stop staring at it. Because I never imagined anything like that could happen, I was understandably shocked when I heard Dad's voice suddenly call out, "Wonderful weather we're having!"

When the man's potted plant responded in the voice of an elegant lady—"Yes, we sure are"—I was seized with such shock that a strange choked noise escaped my throat. The man was stupefied as well, for he stood there with his mouth still full of sandwich, looking back and forth between the two potted plants, then turning his gaze on me with the bewildered expression of someone demanding an explanation.

"I'm sorry… It's my dad…" I stammered, realizing how ludicrous I sounded.

"I see," the man replied, as if my answer was sufficient enough. This time, I peered up at him with a quizzical look on my face, and the man said, "Well, this is my mother," gesturing at the plant.

"I see," I said.

Then, like a magician unveiling a new prop for his enraptured audience, the man brought out another sandwich wrapped in plastic. He asked me if I wanted some and I nodded, seeing that it was a salmon sandwich—my favorite. Accepting the sandwich, I quickly gobbled it down.

From that day on, the four of us met in the same place at the same time almost every day. I learned that the man went by the name P, that he preferred to be called simply P, that he loved to draw, which also happened to be his job, and that his illustrations were usually featured in children's books and magazines, and he smoked menthol, and he preferred weak lattes, and he was a cat person.

Dad also became more talkative whenever he was around P's mother. Sometimes, when his dad jokes hit the mark, P's mother laughed heartily, and each time she did, P and I exchanged knowing looks. Sometimes, I suggested to P that we go for a walk by ourselves and leave the grown-ups to their thing, and when we returned from our long walks, Dad would get annoyed at us for returning so soon and I noticed that the edges of the young leaves on P's mother had turned pink.

One day, P invited us to their home for dinner so Dad and I could enjoy a night out. I wore a new dress and bought a bottle of sweet port wine for P and a solid brick of German-made plant fertilizer for his mother, which was said to be good for up to ten years. Dad wanted to look his best that night and remained obedient as I sheared off some of his wild overgrowth with the dreaded pair of clippers. As a result, he looked nice and clean by the time we arrived at P's house.

When P opened the door, we were met by a gust of warm kitchen steam and an overpoweringly delicious smell that lifted my spirits even before I'd entered the house. P's apartment was structured like ours, with a small living room that opened to a balcony and an even smaller bedroom. I fell in love with the place at first sight. It was clear P had rushed around tidying up in advance of his guests' arrival, but I still noticed the swirls of dust piled up in the corners, the handprints on the glass windows, and the scratches on the linoleum. When I remarked upon these endearing human touches all over his cozy home and said how much I loved them, P blushed.

P had set a table for four, and we sat facing each other across the table—P facing me and my father facing his mother. P filled four wine glasses, two with the port wine I'd brought and another two with mineral water. Handing me the glass with the wine and pouring the other glass of water over my father, P cracked a corny joke about drinking in moderation that wasn't all that funny but nevertheless made my dad shake his leaves with laughter. I feasted on the food that was before me, which P seemed to materialize out of thin air and ladled onto empty plates. When all the pots had been emptied, P, scratching the back of his head, muttered something about being out of cigarettes, and even before he could ask, I found myself standing by the front door, digging my feet into my shoes.

It was a spring night and the air smelled of fresh lilac blossoms. P said that he imagined there were lilac trees planted somewhere near the apartment building but that he was never able to track them down, to which I nodded and said, *I see*. Neither of us spoke for a while. We walked to the convenience store around the corner and bought cigarettes. I expected the walk back would also involve silence but before we arrived, P glanced at the rows of shrubs planted near the building, as if looking for the missing lilacs, then murmured quietly, "How would you like to go out with me?"

"Okay, sure," I said.

When I told my dad this the next day, he exclaimed that it was fantastic news. Then, suddenly changing the subject, he remarked on how fine the weather was these days. I realized that he must have asked P's mother the same question while we were away and that P's mother must have given the same answer as me.

Neither P nor I was a big fan of gallivanting out and about so we spent most of our time at his place. P's apartment was full of the drawing tools he used for work, which I used to doodle or twirl as I read comic books while watching P work. His illustrations were warm and inviting just like he was, rich with soft, dewy colors that shined brilliantly on the thick white paper he used. I could never get tired of watching him work. P would sit and draw for hours on end, pausing for brief moments to complain of hunger or his stiff shoulders. When he did, we cooked up a meal or headed out for a short walk.

Dad and P's mother would spend their days just as lazily, unfurling their stems to stretch them out over one another as they basked in the sun during the day and relaxed at night. I sometimes caught my dad and his thick, rough leaves tenderly stroking P's mother and her small, round ones and blushed to myself for having witnessed such a scene.

P and I became chattier in bed right before going to sleep. On the ceiling above the bed, P had stuck several glow-in-the-dark stars a long time ago, and it was underneath those stars that we shared many long conversations. When I told P about the fateful day I almost drowned and how Dad kept going back to that story every time he wanted a favor, P laughed uproariously, kicking off the covers in the process. When I begged him to tell me more about his mother, P thought hard about what to say before launching into an anecdote from when he was eight years old. He and his mother were at a shopping mall when he began begging her for a new toy robot. Annoyed, his mother dragged him to the cashier's desk, then, thrusting him at the lady at the cash register, shouted that he could stay with her if he liked toy robots so much, before marching home by herself. P shrugged and thought, *Might as well*, then waited for the lady to finish work before following her home and having dinner there. He stayed up for a while watching cartoons before going to bed, then, when the lady got up the next morning to go to work, he got up as well and took the bus home while the lady went back to the store. At this, I laughed so hard my stomach started tickling. As I closed my eyes and dozed off to sleep, I heard my dad and P's mother murmuring to each other on the balcony. Their gentle conversation, along with the light breeze flowed into our room and rocked me to sleep as if it were a soft lullaby.

The next morning, I got up and wandered out to the balcony where Dad and P's mother greeted me warmly with their leaves folded over one another. I began the day by pouring half a cup of lukewarm tap water over each of their pots.

Dad and P's mother grew steadily closer and edged nearer to one another so that, not long after, their branches became intertwined to the point they appeared to be of the same tree and it became all but impossible to wrench them apart from one another. Unless you looked very closely, you could hardly tell them apart (not that there was any need to do so). As P and I were similar to one another and so were Dad and P's mother, the four of us were steadily becoming more and more alike, which wasn't such a bad thing.

One evening, P was lounging in the living room reading my translation of the story *Apple*, and I was thinking about suggesting we snack on some dried ramen noodles when I heard my father call out to us.

"Kids, will you come here for a minute?"

After exchanging looks, P and I headed out to the balcony.

"What do you want this time?" I huffed, to which P shot me a stern look.

Ignoring me, Dad spoke in a low, solemn voice. "We are getting married."

I stole a glance at P and saw that he was struggling to contain his laughter. I, for one, decided to let loose. P jabbed me in the ribs and told me to stop, and I did so abruptly. Since I'd had a good laugh nonetheless, I asked, "Why?"

"Because we're about to have a child," Dad answered instantly, as if he'd been waiting to break this news.

I suddenly had visions of the fictional Mandrake plant that erupts into loud wails when you pull it from the earth, then of Baby Groot from the film *Guardians of the Galaxy Vol. 2*. I couldn't imagine what the "child" would look like, then began giggling again at how silly my dad was being. It turned out that the "child" my dad spoke of looked nothing like what

I'd vaguely imagined. When P gently smoothed some of the leaves out of the way, we could see a small, round flower bud that was firmly closed, with a pointed tip.

Shyly, P's mother murmured, "I think she'll blossom sometime in the next two days."

P and I looked at each other.

"Congratulations, I guess," P said awkwardly, and his expression was so funny that I collapsed into another fit of giggles.

On the day of our parents' wedding, P and I went to the flower market and bought the biggest, most eye-catching pot there, then carefully moved Dad and P's mother over to the new pot. I put on a pretty dress and P wore his suit. We sat around the kitchen table, lit some candles on a cake, and toasted over glasses of champagne.

"This doesn't feel a wedding. This is more like a birthday," Dad complained. But I thought it was fun. Feeling sentimental, I pretended to wipe away tears and said in a fake whisper, "So this is what it feels like to send your son off," and made everyone laugh.

In bed that night, I turned to P and said, "Do you realize we're brother and sister now?"

"Well then, let's do something siblings should never do," P coaxed. We ended up sharing a night that made the glow-in-the-dark stars in the ceiling blush and fall off, although in fact they fell because I'd pounded on the wall. The next morning, the entire house was full of the heavily sweet scent of yellow pollen from the pink flower bud that had blossomed during the night.

After the flower wilted and fell, there was a small, red fruit in its place.

Dad and P's mother didn't appear to talk very much after that, but I still caught one of them giggling softly or trembling with mirth from time to time. It seemed they didn't have to give voice to their feelings anymore, which wasn't surprising, as they were one and the same tree now.

The little fruit grew bigger and bigger as the months passed, so that what used to be as small as a button grew to the size of a piece of peppermint candy, then to a rice cake the size of one's palm with a shiny, firm peel. I thought I caught it shifting and moving sometimes. When I stroked the fruit with the end of my finger, I felt its soft, pulpy insides, which was quite cute. Every day I poked and prodded the fruit, wondering if it was ripe yet. I spoke to it and waited.

Once it had deepened to a dark red color and grown to the size of a baby bunny, it finally happened.

"She's coming, she's here!" P's mother cried out. P and I hurried over to the balcony. The surface of the fruit was quivering, and it was clear the fruit was trying hard to dislodge itself from the stem. Then, so suddenly that we had no chance to shout out loud, the fruit broke free from the tree and rolled away on the floor. It was headed underneath the couch but P managed to grab it just in time.

"She's warm," P said.

I reached out and P gently placed the fruit in my palm. She really was warm, and although it was without any eyes or nose or lips or any discernible features, I thought it was the cutest thing ever and felt a strong urge to rub it against my cheek. I gave the fruit back to P.

"What are we going to do with it?" P wondered, as he rolled the fruit in his palm.

That's when I realized I'd only given thought to the fruit's birth and never considered what we were going to do with it after she arrived. Frowning, I met P's gaze.

The fruit remained silent and still in P's palm. Carefully, P carried it over to the kitchen table, placed a towel on the surface, and laid the fruit on it. With the fruit between us, P and I discussed what to do with it. If we didn't do something soon, the fruit was going to go bad and rot. But we didn't want to bury the little thing straight away in the soil, either. When we asked our parents, they said they'd leave the decision up to us, as the fruit was our little "sibling" after all. For a while, we discussed various ideas, prodding and stroking the fruit on the table. Suddenly, P stood up and brought out a small paring knife from one of the drawers.

"Let's just cut it open and eat it."

I didn't think that was such a bad idea. When P brought the knife to the fruit, its soft peel immediately gave way to a red, pulpy flesh that looked quite mouth-watering. P and I each grabbed a small piece and, on the count of three, tossed it into our mouths. The fruit was juicy and its scent overpoweringly sweet. Pleasantly surprised, we nodded to one another and chewed diligently. When at last I swallowed, I felt the pulpy mess course down my throat and could picture it plunking into my stomach to get absorbed along with everything else in there.

That night, I had a strange dream. In it, I was running around what looked to be a closed amusement park, chasing after a red ball that was constantly rolling away from me.

When I finally managed to grab the ball and tuck it into my pocket, I woke up. When I told P about the dream the next morning, he wondered aloud whether the dream meant I was going to have a baby soon.

"Huh, maybe," I said.

DRIFTING

Two lights were shining far away in the distance. The lights changed color constantly, fading from red to pink to green to yellow then back to red again. I forced myself to keep my eyes open and catch the precise moment the lights changed color but it was no use. No matter how hard or how long I stared, they remained elusive. *Forget it*, I thought.

Instead, I decided to focus on my feet. I'd lost all feeling below my shoulders way earlier, but I should've been kicking my feet as hard as I could. I wanted to reach down and touch my feet to see whether they were really treading water, but any slight change from my position would complicate my situation. I had no choice but to trust that my feet were still moving and instead continued staring at those lights. But the lights were getting smaller. Definitely smaller. They used to be as big as my thumbnail. Now they were smaller than the nail on my pinky. But at least I could still tell the colors apart. Red, pink, green, yellow, back to red again. The lights were definitely turning red in the inky blackness. Seeing red comforted me somehow.

Red is Mok Hyung-gyu's signature color.

I realize this sounds ludicrous. Why care about the color red in my current situation? Most people might think me insane. I knew those lights weren't coming from light-sticks or huge balloons waved by fans at a concert stadium but that they were flashing from the tallest pier of Incheon Bridge. But if you're in love, you're bound to see the person you love in every moment and in everything you see, even if you're bobbing along the surface of the ocean somewhere in the pitch dark of night.

That's right. I am drifting somewhere in the West Sea. Clutching a newly released, limited edition, 85-liter, fire engine-red Rimowa x Supreme collaboration suitcase as if it were a buoy.

I bought this luggage for Hyung-gyu's twenty-first birthday. It was a stroke of genius to have chosen this as his birthday gift. When my car crashed through the guardrail and plummeted over the bridge, the suitcase had shattered the window but had made it to the sea without a scratch to its polycarbonate body. It remained firmly leakproof in the water. All that legwork and hard work to get this piece of luggage was paying off big time. I say legwork and hard work because it was definitely not easy. The suitcase was completely sold out in Korea, so I had to email different sellers in Canada, the U.S., and even Vietnam until I finally managed to track down someone with the merchandise. Then I had to beg and plead at the seller to make sure the suitcase would arrive in time for Hyung-gyu's birthday. Not to mention the exorbitant price I had to cough up. Rimowa suitcases weren't exactly cheap to begin with, but slap one with the red Supreme logo and the price jumped to several times the original ASP. I don't want to mention any numbers, but suffice it to say the suitcase was equivalent to several semesters' worth of tuition at an average private university. But the price ceased to become an issue when I imagined Hyung-gyu's delighted face upon being presented with this gift. Hyung-gyu's smile was a million-dollar smile.

A million dollars is roughly equivalent to 1.2 billion Korean won. This means I owed Hyung-gyu 1.2 billion won, and I had a long way to go before I could pay off that debt. Although the suitcase probably brought the debt down to about half what it was.

Even if I were to drown tonight, I still longed to deliver this gift to Hyung-gyu. He'd start squealing like a little puppy the second he saw me rolling in the suitcase, quickly deducing it was meant for him. *Noona, thank you so much! Wow, how'd you know I wanted that?* he would say, feigning innocence. And to that I'd say, *How'd I know? You talked about wanting a new suitcase on your Instagram Live. Don't ever do that again. What if it clashes with a sponsor's merch? If there's anything you want, just let Noona know.* With that, I'd hand the suitcase to a grinning Hyung-gyu, turn, and walk away. If I didn't play it cool, the moment would be lost. I'd have to go back to the dormitory and get ready for the next day anyway. Make sure the camera batteries are fully charged. Memory cards all emptied out. Check and double check the subway route to the concert venue. There could be no mistakes. It was the first day of Mok Hyung-gyu's world tour. Mok Hyung-gyu, the K-pop superstar. My job was to take the most breathtaking pictures for his fans and for posterity. I was planning to click the shutter like crazy, enough to shatter the frames, and painstakingly Photoshop the pictures so that every single hair on his head, every single speck of dust flying in the air, would be given due justice.

Although now experienced enough to remain unfazed before run-of-the-mill performances, Hyung-gyu appeared nervous about the upcoming world tour. It was his first solo international concert, but tickets weren't selling as quickly as we'd hoped. The media was having a field day of course, debating what this meant about Hyung-gyu's first world tour. Some articles were quick to pronounce that his career would be placed on life support if he didn't deliver at this concert. Hyung-gyu had screen-grabbed that article and sent it to me. *Noona, I'm going to shut this guy down!* Moved by how much he'd matured, I trembled as I clutched my phone close. Then his next message. *To do that, I'm gonna need your help. Will you help me, Noona?*

I typed back. *Of course. Just tell me what you need.*

And I meant what I said. I was willing to do anything for Hyung-gyu. I bought a box of chocolate muffins from Costco. I cut the muffins into halves and hid little baggies of marijuana covered in shrink-wrap inside the soft buns. I vacuum sealed the whole lot to make sure no smell escaped then placed hologram stickers reading ♥ Mok Hyung-gyu ♥ over the muffins to make them seem like just another gift from a lovelorn fan before packing them inside the suitcase.

I have to get these to Hyung-gyu, fast.

His plane must have taken off by now. It broke my heart to think of how Hyung-gyu must be waiting for these muffins, feeling crushed under the pressure of the concert. I knew drugs were bad, but he said he needed the weed to take the edge off. What if I end up ruining the concert?

I might as well drown right here.

I knew I had to stay alert but I was getting sleepy. My body temperature was falling dangerously low from the icy water. I remembered how in disaster movies the survivors would yell at each other to stay awake, because once they went to sleep, it was over. No, I can't let that happen to me. I summoned my last remaining strength to sing the entire track list of Hyung-gyu's first solo album. *Nanana, nana nanana, love comes like summer rain, nanana, nana, na.*

The lights from the pier were much too far away now. Almost like the distance between Hyung-gyu and me. Every time I stared at something far off in the distance, I thought of Hyung-gyu. Hyung-gyu, who shined so bright yet was so far away, whom I couldn't bear to hold let alone reach out for. Not that I wanted to hold him. I knew the second I fell for him that he would forever remain out of my grasp. I was happy simply to drift along where I was, where I could see the lights. If only I could make it out alive to send this suitcase to Hyung-gyu. Holding it close, I stared hard at the tiny lights, now just specks in the distance, as they blinked at me. Each time they turned red, I started singing again. *Nanana, nana nanana...*

I can never forget that summer I first met Hyung-gyu.

It was six years ago, on a day so blisteringly hot that the asphalt on the road practically stuck to the soles of my rubber sneakers. I was in art school, working on my graduation piece in Western art. On that day, I was on my way to the Homi Art Shop near Hongik University to grab more art supplies. I was about to turn into a picturesque alley when I saw a kid dancing in the heat, having taken over an entire sidewalk. The sun was so oppressively hot that there was no audience to speak of, which made him stand out even from where I was. He was short with bleached blond hair and black roots, wearing red Supreme Air Force Ones and silver crosses that dangled from his ears every time he moved. The small speaker in front of him was blasting the phenomenally popular *Scary Monsters and Nice Sprites* EP by Skrillex. The boy jerked, swung, and moved to the music as if he were possessed. I stood rooted to the spot, watching him dance. He was dancing so wildly that only after the music had ended and he had stopped dancing could I study his face closely. His face was flushed red and covered in sweat. Gasping for breath, he slumped to the ground. I immediately felt an indescribable urge to run to the convenience store nearby and buy a cup of ice along with a bottle of water. I poured water into the cup and ran back to where he was.

"Here, drink this. Otherwise you're going to pass out."

The portable speaker was already playing the next song. But the boy didn't dance. He looked up at me, then at the cup of ice water, then back at me, in the blazing summer heat.

"Is that for me?" he asked. I nodded. I didn't think what I'd done was a big deal, but suddenly, the kid's lower lip began to tremble. Tears formed in his big, double-lidded eyes and fell down his cheeks.

"Thank you, Noona. Seriously. Thank you. So much."

He was clutching the cup with both hands, his head bowed low. Every time his shoulders heaved, sunlight bounced off his blond hair.

Stumbling, I backed away. It wasn't that I was shocked at his unexpectedly strong reaction or that I was uncomfortable at having a stranger openly sob in front of me. Rather, I was overwhelmed by a powerful wave of dizziness that washed over me as if someone had pounded my head with a hammer.

Fans of K-pop stars refer to this moment as "stan start," the split second in time when their star worship begins, as if it was a stroke of cosmic fate that brought them together with their favorite celebrity. But I didn't feel that expression did my experience—and the explosion of emotions I felt—enough justice. In that very moment, I knew I would devote the rest of my life to this kid. It was as clear as if my own guardian angel had whispered these words to me. I was going to risk my life and everything I knew for this kid—from the pair of ears flushed red from the heat to the hands clasped tightly around the cup to his almond-shaped fingernails.

Like some wild, hunted animal, I whipped my head around to check out the surroundings. I saw a small sign set up next to the speaker.

15-YEAR-OLD MOK HYUNG-GYU,
ASPIRING, UNDISCOVERED STAR!
YOUR SUPPORT IS MUCH APPRECIATED

Next to the sign sat an empty, open guitar case with a couple of crumpled bills and a few coins scattered inside. I glared at the measly contents. *From now on, that case will only hold the largest bills. I will make sure of that*, I vowed to myself as the boy continued to stand before me, sweating and sobbing.

Nothing was going to stop me.

There were several clear pieces of evidence that proved Hyung-gyu and I were destined to be together, one of which was that we shared the same last name. The surname Mok is one of the rarest in Korea, with only 9,000 living Koreans with that last name. I personally had never come across anyone else in my life, other than the relatives on my dad's side, who shared that last name. But it just so happened that Hyung-gyu was a Mok. This wasn't mere coincidence.

Before I met Hyung-gyu, I wasn't fond of my last name. Actually, that would be an understatement. As a young girl, I would have done anything to change it. Being a shy introvert who hated attracting attention to herself, this was the worst surname to have. Any time I introduced myself to strangers as Mok Un-tak, invariably the response would be, "What? What kind of name is that for a girl?" Things got worse when I started school. Boys would run up to me, karate chop me on the back of my neck, and yell, "Haha, *tak* goes your *mok*!" before running away, laughing over what they thought was a hilarious play on words as *mok* was the Korean word for "neck." Instead of chasing after them, however, I'd crumple to the floor and burst into tears. I could cope with the crude name Un-tak but why was I cursed with the last name Mok? Of all the pretty surnames in Korea, why this?

If my father had been the affectionate type, I might have playfully complained about the name and hinted at possibly changing it. But if I were to rank all the Korean men with the last name Mok on the affectionate scale, my dad would come in dead last. He was not a man with feelings. In fact, I can't remember my dad ever hugging me, and I was his only daughter. My most vivid memory of him is his face half-covered by the morning paper, as I sat across from him at the breakfast table. Then he'd get up, leave for work, and return late at night. If I were to cry or whine in his presence, he would shut me up at once.

"Make her be quiet," he would command my mother in a cold, calm voice, as if he were a passing stranger.

But it wasn't that my dad didn't love me. He just loved me in his own way. And his way was simple. It involved money, lots and lots of money, which was possible because Dad was a senior executive at a large conglomerate. I attended one of the best private kindergartens in Seoul then went on to a private elementary school and private middle school. When I said I wanted to major in art, Dad rented out a studio and hired a private tutor who had gone to Seoul National University. Although it took two tries, I managed to get into the school I wanted, Hongik University, and when I did, Dad purchased a large unit in a new apartment near my campus, under my own name—along with a brand new, bright yellow Mini Cooper.

If I had decided to go to Samik Shop for my art supplies run instead of Homi, or chosen not to head out at all and ordered the supplies online instead, I wouldn't have run into Hyung-gyu and consequently would have submitted my graduation piece on time, left university, then gone abroad to study. I would have traveled across Europe, drawing whatever I fancied, then returned to Korea once I got bored. I might have married a man from a similar background, got married, and maybe even had a kid. I'd have set up a small studio of my own, maybe held a few solo exhibitions from time to time and lived the life of a part-time artist with her long, curly hair tied up in a determined ponytail.

But even then, I'd have hated my last name.

After Hyung-gyu came into my life, however, I came to truly love not just him, but myself as well. I was a person worthy of love, for I shared the same last name as Hyung-gyu. I helped to make Hyung-gyu shine, and this in turn made me worthy. Mok Un-tak had value only when she was with Mok Hyung-gyu. Listening to his music sent jolts to the tips of my fingers and toes. When he smiled, the whole world seemed to melt. At the same time, he and I seemed to be one and the same lovable, luminescent presence. If my body were to be completely dismantled and carefully put back together piece by brilliant piece, it would form Hyung-gyu. I felt alive only when I was doing something for Hyung-gyu and believed this was the reason we were put on Earth at the same time. My mandate was to provide tons of nutrition and water and sunlight to this small sapling that was Hyung-gyu. I felt like I was truly myself only when I was with him. Like the light side of the moon that is only as bright as the sun it reflects—for me to make something of my life meant that I had to make something of his. I had no choice but to love him wholeheartedly.

I gave up working on my nearly completed graduation piece. Instead, I began drawing Hyung-gyu. Hyung-gyu dancing, Hyung-gyu chattering, Hyung-gyu nodding off to sleep. I hadn't felt so inspired to paint since I first took this up as a discipline. I uploaded my lovingly finished paintings to the website of Hyung-gyu's official fan club, which I had created and which at the time had only two members—myself and Hyung-gyu. Still, Hyung-gyu commented on all the new paintings I uploaded. *This is so amazing, Noona! Is this really supposed to be me? I look BOMB! I'm gonna work to live up to this, Noona. Will you be with me till then?*

Of course, I will. I will be with you to the very end.

The first possession I sold was the Mini Cooper. It wasn't a big deal because I rarely used the car anyway. With the money, I bought an expensive camera and a lens shaped like a cannon typically used to take professional photographs of migratory birds. Every other week, I rented out a concert hall so Hyung-gyu could perform on stage solo. Instead of the cramped, hourly studio Hyung-gyu was used to practicing in, I paid for a more spacious, private rehearsal studio and hired a famous choreographer, vocal trainer, and personal fitness coach to whip him into shape. I got Hyung-gyu a new guitar, bass guitar, drum set, cello, and violin along with any other instrument he wanted to learn. Each time we met, I gifted him with the most popular new things—the latest gaming device, designer puffer coats, a laptop computer. Soon, I ran out of money. But I wasn't concerned. There were always ways to come up with more money. I sold the condo that was in my name and decided to rent a small studio apartment instead. I paid for the rent with the allowance my parents gave me. I had to come up with increasingly elaborate excuses each time my mom offered to come visit me with a home-cooked meal, but things somehow worked out. I didn't care, so long as Hyung-gyu was happy, so long as Hyung-gyu could become the famous artist he wanted to be.

Hyung-gyu and I grew increasingly close. I wanted to learn everything there was to know about him, and Hyung-gyu gladly told me all about his life. He told me how he had lost his parents when he was still a baby and how he was raised by his grandparents. He told me how, in grade school, he told his crush how much he loved her in front of the whole school and was completely rebuffed. He told me that music and P.E. were his favorite subjects. He told me what his current favorite mobile game was. Hyung-gyu was younger than me and had a babyish personality that meant he looked up to me as he would an older sister. This relationship thrilled me. After all, I would never have considered Hyung-gyu to be a possible romantic interest, even if there wasn't an age difference. He was like a beautiful wild animal. And just how animals are meant to be loved by being fed fresh food and given plenty of room to roam around in, I wanted to provide a safe and secure environment for Hyung-gyu. That was more than enough.

I remember the night I gifted him a new scooter. When he begged me for one, I told him to get a motorcycle license first, which he did and proudly flaunted the next time we met, leaving me with no choice but to buy him the scooter. Ignoring my pleas to drive safely, Hyung-gyu became lost in his own world, stroking the bright red Honda for a long time before suddenly lifting me up and placing me on the back.

"I want you to be the first one on it."

Revving the engine, he began racing down an empty freeway in the middle of the night. I squealed in terror and grabbed Hyung-gyu from behind. I remember how slim and narrow his young body felt. *I could die happy right now*, I thought, my face buried in his sweat-soaked shirt. As I did, the scooter began to sputter and shake then pull to a complete stop in the middle of the road. It had run out of gas. Confused, we stared at each other before bursting out laughing. We laughed and laughed till our stomachs hurt, then dragged the scooter to the nearest gas station.

I still treasure those moments.

Of course, these are moments from the past. Hyung-gyu and I could never share such private moments after he became famous. I was scared people would get the wrong idea about us and start gossiping. Instead, we texted each other all day. Hyung-gyu was always lonely. He texted me late at night every day.

"You up? WYD? Let's talk."

Sometimes, he sent me audio messages of songs he claimed to have written for me. I still have those old, awkwardly sung audio clips stored on my hard drive. He was a kid when he made that music, and most of the songs were about new shiny things he wanted.

What do you get when you take the OE out of LOVE? Lalala, you're left with L and V! Take it out, OE. Take out the bitter stuff. Take out the OE.

Laughing, I'd run down to the nearest Louis Vuitton boutique.

"Here's your silly L and V," I announced. I loved being able to indulge him and his bare-faced requests. I wanted to do this for the rest of my life.

But there was more to what I did than throw money at Hyung-gyu. I analyzed and strategized his situation, calculating the best career moves for us to make. Already 17 years old, Hyung-gyu didn't have much time. He didn't have some of the advantages his competitors had. He hadn't gone to a prestigious school for the arts. He was never hired as a trainee by a big management company. He was just a kid who liked to sing and dance. I knew I needed something big to turn him into a star. But what? I set up a YouTube channel and hosted several meet-and-greets through the fan website I created, but it wasn't enough. Hyung-gyu's skills had improved enormously, and he regularly went to audition for the big entertainment firms but was never called back. I became nervous and Hyung-gyu was getting exhausted.

Then one day, a breakthrough came in the most unexpected way. I was attending a relative's wedding with my parents when I noticed a man who was dressed in a distinct way that made him stand out from the otherwise drab crowd. I asked my mom who that was.

"You don't recognize your uncle?" Mom said. "He's on your father's side. Your father's sister's husband. He adored you when you were little. He's a successful producer now. Sometimes, he even appears on TV."

I felt my heart drop. The gods were winking at me. This. This was it. I waded through the crowd and headed straight to the man.

"Hello, Uncle. It's me, Un-tak. Do you remember me?"

The man looked up and recognized me right away. "Oh, Mok Un-tak! You were tiny the last time I saw you. Look at you, all grown up!"

Smiling broadly, he offered me his hand. I was smiling as well, but when I reached out for the handshake, my hand was cold and trembling. It was like reaching for a lifeline. I couldn't let go of this. This was the lifeline that Hyung-gyu needed.

Uncle turned out to be a successful head producer at a cable TV network, and, as fate would have it, he was working on a new entertainment show. It would be a combination of the popular trends of *mukbang* and home-cooked meals, featuring several celebrities who would be invited to the home of another celebrity who would cook a meal for them which they'd proceed to wolf down. I emailed Uncle about thirty files of music written and sung by Hyung-gyu. The songs were a good mix of bright and fun, hard and serious, funky and cool. Then I called him.

"Hello? Uncle? It's me, Un-tak. Yeah... I just emailed you some songs. Do you think you can maybe play them in the background during your shows? That's all I'm asking for. Please. I'll take care of the rest. I'm not even asking for the artist to be featured in your program. Please, it's just the background music..."

Uncle delivered on what I asked, and more. His show became a total hit, with ratings going over twenty percent one point during the show's run. Hundreds of memes were edited and disseminated by fans and audiences, highlighting a popular actress shoving *bibimbap* in her mouth and a middle-aged star covertly unloosening his belt buckle under the table. And in all these memes, Hyung-gyu's songs were playing in the background. I spent nights surfing the web and commenting on every link and page I could find, assuming multiple identities.

Whose song is this in the background? I like it.

- ▸ *It's by this new artist, Mok Hyung-gyu! OMG. Am super obsessed. He's on YouTube.*
- ▸ *He's super cute and an awesome dancer. Check him out.*

The work was ridiculous, but effective. As Hyung-gyu's songs began to grow in popularity, other shows picked up the songs and started playing them as well. Hyung-gyu's YouTube channel swelled with more and more subscribers. Seemingly overnight, he came to command a fanbase. The paintings I drew of him were shared and went viral. I monitored almost all the online pop music boards to see how the market was reacting so I could determine our next move. I wanted to see what exactly it was about him that appealed to his fans. What did they like? What did they find off-putting? I thought Hyung-gyu's principal appeal was his cute, playful, boy-next-door demeanor, but it turned out that his fans preferred his story as a sweet, hardworking kid who hoped to make it big. It was a good narrative. A young kid with big dreams who was willing to overcome all odds to achieve his goal.

That was just the beginning. Hyung-gyu soon landed a spot as a guest on a cable TV show and soon began appearing in the major network programs. He performed live on stage for a music broadcast. He received calls from two indie music labels but I advised him to turn them down. Hyung-gyu was aching to ink a contract, *any* contract, but I remained calm. Lion cubs do not belong in a bird's nest. I urged Hyung-gyu to dream big.

"You shouldn't settle. You need to go bigger. You have it in you to go big."

It was around this time when Hyung-gyu first turned to weed.

Initially, I thought he was dating someone behind my back. I became suspicious of how he kept asking me for more and more money when I was already satisfying his every need. He started making excuses to bow out of lessons and stay home. *You seeing someone?* I asked, to which he'd shake his head and vehemently deny the accusation, but my suspicions lingered. I didn't have it in me to get mad at him. Instead, I tried to coax and cajole him, and when that didn't work, I went to see him late one night and demanded he come outside. When he did, his eyes were bloodshot and a distinct smell was enveloping him. The second I took a whiff of that sickly sweet, earthy smell, I knew.

"Hyung-gyu, you're..."

Awkwardly, Hyung-gyu patted me on the shoulder. "I only smoke it every now and then... I know a guy who hooks me up from time to time. If you don't like it, I'll stop. Please don't cry, Noona."

Of course, he didn't stop. He claimed he smoked a joint or two only when the anxiety got to be too bad for him. But the more successful he became, the more he smoked. After craving fame and success for so long, getting it came with the anxiety of knowing that someday he might lose it all. When the call came from a major entertainment label asking him to come in for an audition, when he was set to join a band that was about to make their debut, when their band was about to go on their first live network performance, Hyung-gyu hit the pipe. *I'm so anxious, Noona. I'm so anxious I could die.* Whenever he begged me for more cash, I knew what he was going to use it for. But I also knew that if I denied him the money, he would find someone else to borrow it from or worse, resort to selling his stuff for the cash which would arouse more suspicion.

If I were really honest with myself, however, I never actively tried to get him to quit.

After his debut, Hyung-gyu amassed a small yet fiercely loyal fanbase, of which several turned out to be insanely committed. They camped out all night outside his house to catch a glimpse of him and made pilgrimages to his elementary and middle schools. But none of them knew about his pot habit. This was a secret only Hyung-gyu and I shared, and that made the secret all the more delicious. And while I would never think to do it, I knew I had the power to potentially reveal this explosive secret and ruin everything Hyung-gyu had worked for his entire life. It was horrible to think of, but to be honest, I found myself sometimes—or quite often—imagining such a scenario playing itself out. I imagined Hyung-gyu and I running from the cops after our secret was somehow discovered.

If Hyung-gyu were addicted to drugs, I must have been addicted to this idea—that I somehow held his fate in my hands. I seriously questioned whether, if I could turn back time, I would have stopped him from taking those drugs in the first place. Even now, floating somewhere in the open water, clutching a suitcase full of pot muffins, I wasn't sure I had it in me. I have always believed that I prioritized his integrity and tried to lead him down the correct path, and yet I had deliberately failed to hold him back from his habit and was now on the brink of drowning without having had the chance to deliver this last batch of weed to him. Which was worse?

I wasn't sure.

How far away was I? I couldn't see the blinking lights anymore. No matter where I looked, I was confronted by a vast inky black sea that spread as far and wide as a stretch of black plastic tarp. Only the moon, when it wasn't covered by clouds, cast a feeble gleam over the water. I couldn't hear the sound of the waves, much less any signal from a rescue boat. I had long ago lost the strength to sing. I had succumbed to the motion of the sea, bobbing up and down with the waves.

I could make one of two choices.

The first was to hang on to the luggage for as long as I could while waiting for a lifeboat that may or may not arrive. Of course, if I were to lose all strength in my arms, causing me to let go of the bag, I would most certainly drown. But that would be followed by something much worse than death. For instance, the search-and-rescue team that would arrive belatedly would discover the luggage and pry it open. The rental car I had driven off the bridge might not be found at first, having sunk to the bottom of the sea, but this candy red luggage would be spotted right away. Its contents would be vigorously searched, meaning it would only be a matter of time before they chanced upon the small bags of marijuana stuffed inside the muffins. And the many stickers slapped on the muffins would alert the authorities to the intended recipient of the pot. A few strands of his hair would be more than enough to test for drugs with the results immediately available. Not only would Hyung-gyu's career be over, he could be sent to prison. Either way, he would never be able to recover.

But the situation wasn't too dire. Because there was also a second option which could prevent the worst from happening. If I could open the luggage and release the pot muffins out to sea, everything would be fine. That way, even if the empty luggage were later recovered, it would be seen as belonging to a dedicated K-pop fan who had been en route to her favorite celebrity's concert before a fateful accident. Hyung-gyu would be free from all blame.

Of course, if I were to do that, I'd be left with nothing to hold on to and would drown immediately.

I'd long since given up attempting to kick my legs and swim. The few ounces of strength I had left were directed completely to my two arms, holding on tightly to the luggage. I felt as if my entire body were composed of just my arms and my head. I'd already lost all feeling in the rest of my body and had no way of telling if it was even there. I didn't have much time left to choose. Should I go for the first option? Or the second? Desperately clinging to what little sense of reason I had, I thought of Hyung-gyu. Of the most brilliant memory I had of him.

Once, Hyung-gyu said that if ever things became tough, we only needed to focus on the most important thing. *Because if it's really the most important thing, nothing else matters*. Hyung-gyu had told me that when he was still an unknown kid, struggling to make it big, when he was still a naïve, glittering young soul who hadn't yet been drawn to drugs. Hyung-gyu, who had kept his eyes on that one shining prize far off in the distance. He was right. I had to treasure and protect that which was most important to me. Hyung-gyu had known that very clear, very simple truth even as a kid. Now I had to know it too, so I could protect him.

Summoning up my last bit of strength, I reached around the side of the luggage until my fingers brushed against the zipper.

★

"I still don't understand. So it *dies* simply from staying in saltwater for a few hours?"

"It's not dead. It's just unconscious."

"Humans are just so…"

"Shhhh! Shut up."

I'd regained consciousness a while ago but I couldn't make out who was talking, much less what they were talking about. Slowly, I opened my eyes and saw that I was lying in a brightly lit white space with no floors or ceiling. It was just an empty, broad stretch of space, set to a temperature that was neither cold nor hot, in a place that seemed to cast no shadows or have any intersecting points. Quite simply, the space didn't seem to belong to our world. *Am I dead?* I wondered. But I didn't *feel* dead. I felt perfectly normal—in fact, better than normal.

"…Hello?" I called out. As I did, the space before my eyes shook then collapsed into concentric circles traveling outward, as if someone had cast a stone into a lake's surface.

"It's awake!"

"You probably woke it up with all your yakking. This… this *woman* should have remained unconscious for at least two more hours, in Earth time."

"So? That just means I saved us time!"

They were the same voices from before. But I couldn't tell where they were coming from. There were no speakers or sound systems piped anywhere, and yet the voices sounded so close as if they were right before me.

"Who's there?" I asked timidly, but I didn't know where to look as I addressed the question.

"Well, hello. How do you feel?" One of the voices asked.

"You're probably feeling quite sprightly," the other voice rushed in. "While we were working on you, we took the liberty of fixing your back and neck, too. Your cervical vertebrae in particular were quite askew. Do you by chance work in a profession that requires long hours of sitting? I can show you a couple of excellent stretches later."

"Those aren't going to work on humans," said the other voice.

I still couldn't comprehend what was going on, but I tried moving my hips a little. It did feel a little better, although I could have been imagining it.

"This must all feel a little confusing," the first voice continued. "We're… uh… We're… How do I explain who we are?"

"Doesn't matter. It wouldn't understand."

"Yeah, none of the other humans did, either."

The two voices momentarily fell silent. Soon, they began speaking again.

"I guess you can say we're… extraterrestrial life forms."

"We *are* extraterrestrial life forms."

"I know we're from outer space, but it's the 'life form' part that might need a bit of explaining."

"We could try, but then this woman will die of old age."

At that, the two voices erupted in laughter. Taken aback, I lay there and waited for them to stop laughing.

"You see, our physical forms are actually in a place far away from Earth. We were watching you and when we saw that your biological signals had died out, we removed you from the water and brought you here."

"We're members of the Outer Space Bioresearch Association," the other voice continued. "We study various living creatures and beings that exist in the universe. Of the many topics of study, we are especially interested in the survival instincts of different life forms. For your information, the survival instinct of Earthlings is one of the highest in the universe."

"The research is interesting in and of itself, but it can also help us learn more about the optimal living conditions for creatures across the galaxy," began the other voice. "For instance, by studying the first emperor of China, Emperor Qin, and his habit of imbibing mercury in the pursuit of immortality, we were able to learn important insights on the commercialization of environments with metallic gases."

"Of course, poor Emperor Qin lacked the necessary technologies to refine mercury."

"In any case, we are currently in the process of observing the emotions of all Earth-bound entities. We observe the moments when their survival instincts spike, then study their thinking and behavioral patterns leading up to the spike."

"Most creatures tend to display the highest levels of survival instinct right before their death. As did you. But you were… a little special, shall we say."

The voices, which had been speaking at a composed, elegant pace, suddenly stopped. Whoever these aliens were, they seemed to be choosing their next words carefully.

I still didn't understand what was going on. This was not the image of the afterlife I'd pictured, and the voices didn't sound anything like Satan or Saint Peter from the gates of Heaven. Briefly, I considered that maybe I was being pranked for a TV show with a bunch of hidden cameras, but the suspicion soon subsided when I realized I was nothing but the administrator of a K-pop star's website and therefore was not particularly newsworthy. Besides, I still remembered the exact moment of my death. After I managed to open the zipper, water quickly rushed into the luggage. I remember frantically reaching inside the bag and taking out the Ziploc baggies with the pot muffins and tearing the bags open so the muffins could be released out to sea. Only then did I succumb to the water and relax my arms and legs. I was about to say as much when the two extraterrestrial voices began giggling, as if they had read my thoughts.

"No, you're right. You died. But we are equipped with the technology to bring Earthlings back from the dead."

"I don't want to toot our own horns here, but we can do things that humans can't even dream of," snorted the other voice.

"Ah, so now we're getting to the point of our story."

Point? What's the point of all this? As I thought that, one word flashed across my brain like lightning. Hyung-gyu. What happened to Hyung-gyu? How did his concert go? Once again, the voices, having read my thoughts, provided the answers.

"Ah, don't worry about that. The concert went well, just as planned."

"He missed one high note but made it work somehow, in an endearing way."

The concert went well? So is it over already? How many hours had passed in the real world? I didn't know what to think, but I was relieved to hear the concert was a success. *See, Hyung-gyu? You don't need weed to be great*. My heart was about to swell with pride at the thought of how proud Hyung-gyu must be feeling, when suddenly, the two alien voices started shouting in unison.

"Yes! That's it!"

"Did you capture that?"

"Yes! I saved it!"

What are they capturing and saving? Now that the adrenaline pumping through my veins had subsided thanks to the relief of knowing the concert had gone well, it was replaced by annoyance. It sounded like these were alien creatures that were obviously much more advanced than human beings, but that didn't give them the right to keep me confined to a bed and talk about me in a way I simply couldn't comprehend. I sat up cross-legged. As I did, I felt once more how much looser and more comfortable my back was feeling, but I ignored the sensation.

"Listen here, sirs."

Strictly speaking, I didn't know if they were sirs of madams or even if the gender construct was applicable in their case but I was deliberately trying to make them uncomfortable. During K-pop concerts, even as beefy security guards stood guard to make sure nobody could smuggle any cameras inside the venue, I used to breeze past with a massive lens hidden inside my coat. Besides, it sounded like I had already died anyway. What more did I have to lose? It didn't sound like these beings were going to harm me either, though I had no basis for such an assumption.

"Can you explain to me what's going on in a language that a lesser being like myself can understand? I'm starting to lose my patience."

They fell quiet. I stayed quiet too, choosing to wait for them instead.

"You're right," one of them said meekly, after a long pause. "We were wrong."

"Allow us to explain everything from the beginning."

"Remember when we mentioned we're researching the survival instinct of Earth-bound human beings? We're particularly interested in the moment when feelings of altruism overpower one's instinct for survival. For instance, think of the heroes you read about in the newspaper who rush onto the tracks of an oncoming train to save a child, or parents who willingly give their lives to save their children. We believe that this sense of altruism is an important key to unlocking longevity in the lives of our species."

"You referred to yourself as a lesser being, but at least when it comes to altruism, humans are far more advanced than we are. In our language, we don't even have a word for 'altruism.'"

After a beat, the voice continued.

"We have compiled enough case studies to further our research. We collected the brainwaves of many humans in those exact moments when altruism takes over to analyze their emotional state at that time. But in those moments, we always identified small concentrations of… shall we say *impurities*, that were present in their systems along with the altruism. For instance, in the brainwaves of a man who sacrificed himself for his beloved, we identified feelings of guilt, of a need to compensate the lover for the love he received. Or in the brainwaves of a father who gave his life for his daughter, we detected feelings of concern for the wife he was leaving behind."

"In effect, we were trying to find someone who died in the purest altruistic sense, of someone who gave the ultimate sacrifice for no other reason than to protect the interests of the other person. Since we couldn't find any such cases, we were just about to give up."

"Then our radar spotted you."

The voices fell silent again. In the silence, I could sense what they were feeling. They were feeling admiration, even respect.

"You willingly gave up your life for someone else, someone who's not in your immediate family or who you're romantically involved with. You did so with no thought for compensation or any sort of reward, with not a single moment's hesitation. All you did was worry about the other person's well-being, and in fact, debated over which manner of your death would impact him the least. Your brainwaves were so clean, so pure, so beautiful."

"I have a pic of your brainwaves as the background on my communications device," piped up the other voice.

"Not only that, your brainwaves were of immense research value. In fact, the brainwaves we were able to extract from your brain in the moment of your death will advance our research by at least fifty light years."

I realized I had started to relax while listening to these beings, so that instead of sitting up ramrod straight, I was now in a more comfortable, hunched-over position. I couldn't believe the moment of my death in the muddy waters of the West Sea was that impactful, almost as much as how I couldn't believe I was talking to literal aliens. At the same time, I understood what they were trying to say. It was true there was no impurity, no other motive, in my feelings for Hyung-gyu. That fact was my only source of pride, the only shining beacon in my life.

"Thank you for saying that," I murmured, feeling slightly guilty for the anger I had earlier felt. I heard what sounded like the clearing of throats. I didn't know if these beings had necks or throats, but it appeared the sound was their attempt at mimicking the social graces in the world of humans, such as the polite way of accepting one's apology.

One of the voices continued, "Now we'd like to ask you a favor."

"Just so you know," the other voice interjected, "you can refuse if you'd like. Even if you refused us, we wouldn't kill you or otherwise harm you in any way. We'll simply erase all memory of us from your mind and have you safely returned home."

Favor? My heart began to race. These were highly advanced extraterrestrial beings, so they wouldn't ask me for any old favor. What if they asked me to give up an organ for the sake of their research? Or perhaps become a host body for one of them to reside in? As these thoughts raced across my mind, the aliens began to giggle.

"It's not a big deal. We just need your consent to scan your life."

"We actually could do it right now, even without your consent, but we are parties to the Pan-Galactic Treaty on the Protection of the Right to Life of All Creatures. Under the treaty, it is forbidden to scan the lives of a living entity without their consent or without offering appropriate compensation."

"We feel we will truly benefit from scanning your entire life from birth to death, in order to understand the source of the pure version of altruism you've demonstrated. The scan will only take one second. You won't feel any pain. In fact, you won't feel anything at all."

Perhaps worried that I might refuse, they continued hurriedly, "Of course, you won't be doing this for nothing. If you allow us to scan you, we'll grant you one wish."

"It can be any wish at all," the other alien said. "However, your memories of us will be completely wiped, and you'll wake up at home as if nothing had happened, with your wish having been granted."

After they were finished, they fell quiet, waiting patiently for me to reach a decision.

Although I was aware these beings could read my thoughts, I still tried to work out in my mind what had just happened. I didn't know exactly what the scan would entail but it sounded harmless enough. My life had been fully and entirely dedicated to supporting Hyung-gyu, so the scan wouldn't reveal any new information. But that was up to them to decide. And on top of that, I'd get a free wish. This didn't seem like a bad deal. What should I ask for? Could I really ask for anything?

Just then, a voice rushed into my thoughts, "Yes! Anything! Want to become the richest person on Earth? Earthlings tend to like that."

"Or if you'd like, we can change the way you look. We have a brochure of good looking Earthlings you can choose from."

I smiled. These aliens still didn't have a clue about me. Did they really think I was going to ask for money or good looks? I simply had one question.

"This wish, can I ask for someone else's wish to come true? Instead of my own?"

At that, the aliens fell silent. Soon, I heard a strange sound that was different from the voices of the extraterrestrial beings. The sound was of several gears turning at once, or maybe the sound of hundreds or thousands of people whispering inside a big, vast room with a high ceiling. What's going on? I wondered. A long while later, the familiar voice spoke again.

"We apologize for that. We were having a discussion."

"We've only granted wishes to a handful of Earthlings so far, but what you said was a truly rare occurrence. No one has asked if they can have someone else's wish granted instead. Every Earthling we spoke to has asked for their own wish to be granted."

"Your sense of altruism is truly marvelous indeed. But I'm afraid our answer is no. You might feel we should oblige because of your high research potential, but unfortunately, we are only allowed to grant the wish of the person who has consented to let us scan their body."

The voice sounded helpless. I was disappointed as well. I was going to ask that Hyung-gyu be turned into the world's most famous celebrity and superstar, but since that wasn't going to work, I had to become someone extraordinarily influential instead. But what, exactly?

"Fine. Just… give me some time to think," I said.

"Of course," one of the voices said. "Take your time. Oh and, this might help you."

With that, a soft, comfortable sofa with big armrests materialized next to me, along with a small round table. On the table was a glass cup, with a straw sticking out. When I approached the table, I saw that it was a large cup full of iced coffee.

"Apparently, you humans believe that caffeine helps you to think."

When I took a sip, I felt like I was coming alive. The sofa was just the right firmness to sit in and think. I leaned back and started thinking as I sipped the coffee. What should I ask for?

Naturally, the first idea that came to mind was to become the CEO of a major entertainment label. Maybe the owner of a big business that had a presence in different industries, including K-pop, film, TV, and fashion. That would enable me to support Hyung-gyu's career as a K-pop star and also as a movie star or fashion model. But was I cut out to be a businesswoman? I had to admit I wasn't sure. And if I were running a big entertainment label, that would mean I'd have many other celebrities and employees to think of, on top of worrying about the operations and management of a huge company. I could barely stay on top of my own finances, much less run an actual company. I'd probably run the place to the ground. So that was a no. What if I asked for riches beyond my imagination, so that I could support Hyung-gyu to do anything he wanted? But this wasn't a very appealing idea, either. Hyung-gyu had already established himself in terms of his career, so he needed something more, something other than money. So that's going to be a no, too. What if... What if I asked to be made into Hyung-gyu's girlfriend?

"Ahhhhhhh!" I squealed.

"What's wrong?" One of the voices asked in alarm.

"Are you okay?" The other shouted.

They must have been concerned at the sight of me rolling on the floor screaming.

"Oh, I'm fine, I'm fine," I managed. "It's just, I'm so happy."

The voices fell silent. I could sense they were exchanging looks with one another, possibly wondering what on earth was wrong with me. That is, if they indeed had eyes. To calm myself, I crushed several pieces of ice between my teeth. What if I could become Hyung-gyu's girlfriend, the one and only woman in his life he loved more than anything else?

But I shook my head. The idea was so exhilarating that the very thought of it made me want to punch the air ten times a second but I knew having a girlfriend wasn't going to help Hyung-gyu's cause. In fact, for a young K-pop star, having a girlfriend would deal a more lethal blow to his career than being caught with drugs in his possession. I knew this better than anyone. And if the girlfriend in question happened not to be a beautiful actress or an uber-talented genius but a normal rando like myself? Nothing could be more horrible.

So what then should I wish for? I knew there must be an incredible idea but nothing came to mind. It's not every day I got the chance to be granted a wish. I certainly didn't want to waste it on something trivial. What could I become, to make Hyung-gyu happy?

Just then, a brilliant idea popped into my mind.

Why hadn't I thought of this sooner? If something like this were really happening, and I could indeed ask a couple of aliens, this was the only logical wish I could possibly ask for.

"Um, not to interrupt or anything," interrupted the familiar voice. "But are you sure that's what you really want?"

"We're capable of doing so much more, you know, really amazing things!"

"Yes, why don't you give it more thought?"

I sat up on the sofa and smiled. I had to give myself credit for this one, I thought. My brain's still got it!

"This is the only thing I want," I said.

Sensing that I was fully committed to the idea, the voices didn't try to argue. One of them sighed.

"Well, if you insist."

Suddenly, I felt a breeze around me. The air surrounding me began to quiver and shake. The entirely white space turned slightly transparent, giving me a glimpse into what lay beyond. There was a complicated system of pipes and machinery fitted with numerous small lightbulbs, each blinking a different color.

"We've just completed the scan of your life," one of the voices said. "We'd like to thank you one last time. This data will provide us with valuable clues into unlocking technology to increase our average life span."

"I hope you know," continued the other voice, "that somewhere out there in the galaxy, your love was able to prevent the deaths of many beings. Of course, you'll soon forget that all this happened."

"I see. Thank you. This was fun," I said, fully realizing I needn't say anything out loud. But they responded as well.

"Goodbye, Earthling. We wish you well."

"Goodbye. We hope the wish we granted you will make you truly happy."

With that, I felt a tingling sensation spread from the soles of my feet and to the whole of my body. I felt tired, but a pleasant sort of tiredness like the feeling one might feel after managing to take several hundred high resolution photographs of a concert up close with one hand on the camera and the other on the front row of the standing concert, then returning home with a sense of utter satisfaction. I leaned back in the sofa, feeling absolutely sure that if I were to close my eyes and wake up, amazing things would be waiting for me.

Right before I fell asleep, I thought I caught an afterimage of blinking lights. I couldn't tell whether they were the lights off the Incheon Bridge or the lights from the white space I was in.

By force of habit, I found myself searching for the red among the many colorful lights.

★

When I woke up, it was morning.

I woke as if from a pleasant dream but I couldn't remember anything. Still in bed, I stretched my arms and legs. My body felt stiff and my joints creaked as if I'd been sleeping for a century, but, strangely enough, I felt as light as air. How long have I been sleeping? I reached next to me and checked my phone. It was Saturday, a little past ten o'clock. Still on the phone, I checked my to-do list for the day. I had to go to the cleaner's, order bottled water, and go to the art supplies store to pick up materials for my graduation piece. I saw I had received several text alerts about the heat wave that was to suffocate the city that day. I should head over to buy the art supplies first before it gets too hot. I'll stop by the dry cleaners on the way back.

I sat up, still feeling light and breezy. Undressing, I headed into the shower, humming all the while. I was in a good mood. A perfect day for shopping. Maybe I'll head to Hyundai Department Store for some light shopping after I pick up the art supplies. After all, no one said art students should wear only paint-flecked aprons.

I peered into my bathroom mirror with my toothbrush in my mouth. Today felt like it was going to be a good day, full of fun surprises. I didn't know what they'd be, but I could tell they'll be memorable for a long time to come.

BROCCOLI PUNCH

When I woke up and checked my phone, I saw that I'd gotten two texts. One said that Won-jun's right hand had turned into a head of broccoli and the other said that Mal-ja, who lived with Mrs. Ahn Pil-soon, had died. Groggily, I squinted at the phone, going back and forth between the two texts.

Mal-ja was a grey parrot that Pil-soon received from her boyfriend on her sixtieth birthday. The bird was amazing at mimicking human voices and was so smart that it had somehow picked up the nuances of the human language. Mal-ja had turned twenty years old this year, which made it practically middle-aged in parrot years, as the birds only lived to be thirty or forty at the most. Due to her age, Mal-ja had begun eating noticeably less a few weeks ago and could barely sit upright on its perch, even toppling over a few times. I could see its health was failing, and now I learned it had died last night. I read Pil-soon's message again. *MAL-JA DEAD COME PLEASE.* For an obituary, it was fairly dry and straight to the point. Which wasn't surprising, given how the two seemed less like an owner and her pet bird than two loudly swearing enemies whose idea of greeting each other was to ask when they were planning on dropping dead. One of them must have picked up the habit from the other, although it was unclear who. I should hurry to see Pil-soon, but I was also worried about Won-jun's hand. As I lay there weighing the ridiculous idea of splitting myself into two to be in both places at the same time, my phone rang. It was Won-jun.

"Are you still in bed?" he asked sullenly. "My right hand has turned into broccoli."

"I saw your text. What happened?"

"Don't know."

I looked at the clock. It was a little past ten in the morning. "You should get that looked at," I said.

"Yeah."

He fell silent. I could hear his even breathing from beyond the phone. Annoyed, I cleared my throat. Getting worked up about his situation certainly wasn't going to make his hand better, but how could he be so calm? Especially when part of his job meant he had to take excellent care of his body? It sounded like he wasn't planning on going to the hospital by himself, meaning I would have to push and drag him there. Wait, where was the nearest hospital anyway? If your hand turned into broccoli, do you go to an internist or an orthopedist? Just as I was about to ask him, my phone let out a sharp beeping sound. There was another call waiting on the line. It had to be Pil-soon. I laid out a map of the neighborhood in my head and tried to mentally calculate the best route. I'll take Won-jun to the hospital first then head over to Pil-soon's house.

After I hung up, I texted Pil-soon. *Won-jun's hand turned into broccoli. I'll stop by the hospital before I come to see you.* Her reply arrived nearly half an hour later as I was pulling on my jeans. *O NO POOR THING HOW DREDFUL.* I imagined Pil-soon frowning at her phone as she texted those letters with the dead Mal-ja beside her. Mal-ja would look like she'd spring to life the moment she saw me walk into Pil-soon's house, flapping her wings madly and squawking, "Get out of my house, you little bitch!" But alas, the bird would never speak again. Most likely Pil-soon had covered the dead parrot with a handkerchief, the familiar rose-patterned handkerchief that I knew so well. The thought was sobering. I sniffled all the way to Won-jun's house.

When I opened the door, I saw Won-jun lying in the same position, in the very place I had expected him to be.

"Hey."

Instead of getting up, he lifted his right hand, or rather the head of broccoli where his right hand should have been, and waved it around. His face was still calm with the lingering stillness of sleep. Gingerly, I navigated around the islands of garbage and dirty laundry on the floor and headed to the sofa bed where Won-jun was lying on his side. I smelled a whiff of fresh cut grass from him.

"When did this happen?"

"I don't know. I woke up to find myself like this."

I grabbed his right hand and gave it a good look. The skin from the middle of his forearm was a dull green, and the color gradually grew darker towards his hand, with small leaves sprouting here and there. His fingers were green stalks that turned into bunches of florets like so many tightly permed little heads—a perfect head of broccoli. Not only that, it looked incredibly fresh and firm, to the point where I might have eagerly picked it up had I come across it at the grocery store. Amazed, I couldn't help but continuously stroke the thick stalks. It was a majestic specimen of vegetable, and my teeth tingled with the desire to crunch down on the fresh broccoli.

"Wow, this is so cool," I murmured as I continued to stroke the broccoli.

Won-jun grinned, "Cool, right?"

Sensing his tone, which sounded as if he had no intentions to go to the hospital, I shut it down then and there.

"Yeah, it's cool but we have to fix it. We can't leave your hand looking like that."

"Yeah, yeah, let's go."

He acquiesced easily enough.

"Good."

With that, I helped him sit up. I got him dressed in a hooded T-shirt and pants, wet my hands and brushed them through his hair, and finally removed the crust from his eyes. I wrapped his broccoli hand in a big towel so he wouldn't have to be embarrassed as he walked around. As I did so, Won-jun sat still like a stuffed animal and stared at me. I could tell he was about to say something.

But by the time I'd locked the front door, Won-jun was already walking away into the distance. *Hey, wait up!* I yelled. He looked back, his face as serene as before. But on the inside, I'm sure he must be in shock after what happened to his hand. He was pretending to be okay, but I knew he wasn't as I ran to catch up to him.

Ko Won-jun is a boxer. When I introduce him as a boxer, most people respond with, "Oh you don't say?" but give me a look like they don't believe me. That's because Won-jun doesn't have any of the features one might expect from a boxer, say, a tall height or a strong physique or a sharp, menacing look. Won-jun had a round jaw and black, bushy eyebrows that hinted at a rambunctious childhood, and, as an adult, gave the impression of being a mailman or a Chinese food chef if one had to guess his occupation. But if the same people saw him compete in a boxing match, they would have no doubt he was a boxer. As soon as he climbed into the ring and the match began, Won-jun transformed into a completely different person. On the outside, he still looked like the Ko Won-jun I knew, but it was as if he had been replaced by someone else on the inside, someone I didn't recognize at all.

The first and only time I saw Won-jun in a boxing match was a few years ago. I left and went home before the match had ended without telling him I was leaving. For a few days afterward, I let his calls go unanswered. I avoided him because I was terrified. Obviously, I wasn't terrified of the fact that there had been two people in the ring hitting and punching each other. I knew what boxing looked like. Rather, I felt unbearable terror at the raw emotion Won-jun emitted every time he punched his opponent. I could sense malice in every deadly punch he threw, in his footwork aimed to distract his opponent, and in the savage glint of his eyes. Till then, I had never imagined Won-jun to be the kind of person who could harness such deadly energy and hit another person. Others might call it spirit or even passion, but to me, it seemed like malice and nothing more. I felt like I was the opponent he was beating up in that ring, and my heart beat fast and hard at the terror I felt.

I didn't go to any of his matches after that. I couldn't bring myself to tell him I was afraid of him, so instead I came up with a bunch of other excuses. But Won-jun never seemed to mind that I didn't come to his matches, and besides, there weren't that many to begin with.

Even so, I knew enough about Won-jun as a boxer. That much I learned from Pil-soon's boyfriend, Park Gwang-suk. The small, thin-as-a-stick old man was a huge fan of all combat sports including boxing, UFC, and wrestling, and when he learned that Won-jun and I were dating, he became so inconsolably excited that I had to rush over with cold water to help him calm down. It was Gwang-suk who told me about the golden prime of Won-jun's career. The old man talked at length about how Won-jun came out of nowhere as a young upstart with incredible fighting spirit and rushed at his opponents with no intention of ever letting up, and about that one time when Gwang-suk was rooting so hard for him in the audience that he didn't notice how a temporary tooth he had gotten while waiting for an implant had come loose in his mouth. When I asked him what happened to the tooth, he opened his mouth wide and pointed to a slightly less yellow molar in a row of very yellow molars. "I swallowed it," he said. Gulp. At that, Pil-soon and I—and Gwang-suk, too—laughed so hard we had to struggle to breathe and didn't get to hear the end of the story of Won-jun in his prime, so I decided to look him up on the internet after I came home. I found everything I could on his career, including information about his time as an up-and-coming amateur boxer who achieved consecutive wins before experiencing a slump, as well as an interview he gave where he revealed his training routine and weight loss secrets. I enjoyed reading them all. But I couldn't believe that the stories were about my boyfriend.

Although I liked to tell Won-jun all about the elderly patients I took care of as a long-term care nurse, Won-jun never told me anything about his work. When I asked him why, he said there was nothing to talk about. It's always the same thing—training, sparring, losing weight, he had said, still looking more like a Chinese food chef than a professional boxer. I asked him if he liked boxing. For a while, he didn't respond. Then he sucked in air through his nose and let out a snort, which I took for an answer and thought to myself, *I shouldn't have asked*. He was fairly talkative about all other things and liked to talk about himself as well, so it was strange that he clammed up when it came to his career. I had to admit that I myself didn't get into long-term care because I was crazy about the profession. Just as how I might not like everything there was to like about long-term care but still enjoyed keeping company with patients like Pil-soon, Won-jun must not have liked everything about boxing but still enjoyed some parts of it. Although I wondered whether the parts he enjoyed included beating people up. That was the one question I really wanted to ask him, but of course I never said it out loud.

I took Won-jun to a clinic I had seen near an overpass, not because we wanted to go to that particular place but because I remembered I'd seen it before when I passed the street it was on. But when we arrived, we saw that the sign outside read FAMILY MEDICINE. I didn't know if a family medicine doctor could help with a broccoli hand. Unsure of what to do, we stood there looking at each other until a voice called out to us from inside the hospital asking us to come in. So we did. Inside the small lobby a few moms sat here and there on the couches with their kids, their faces flushed and red. A nurse sitting behind the counter looked up at us with a friendly smile.

"How can I help you today?" The nurse directed her question at me, thinking that if she had to guess which one of us was the patient, it would most likely be me. I removed the towel from Won-jun's hand and showed her the stump of broccoli.

"His hand is a little . . ."

Seeing Won-jun's hand, the nurse let out a sharp gasp. At that, the sick kids and their moms, who had been distracted by the TV and their phones, instantly turned to look at us. When they saw the broccoli, they all began gasping and reacting in turn, so that the entire lobby became as loud and confusing as an open-air market. "Oh my gosh, I haven't seen a broccoli like that in years! You know what, my father-in-law had that happen to him, too. His broccoli is huge! Oh he must be so uncomfortable!" Blushing intensely, Won-jun grabbed the towel and hurriedly wrapped it over his hand. With a smile, the nurse handed us a form to fill out. When I wrote Won-jun's address and phone number then handed it back to her, the nurse wrote *Broccoli, right hand* on the top right corner of the form in neat, round letters. Then we sat on the sofa and waited our turn.

"You're so young to have something like that happen to you," smiled a kindly woman sitting across from us. A little boy with a runny nose, who was probably her grandson, was lying across her lap.

"You must have a lot on your mind," someone else spoke up.

"Yes, yes, that happens when you have too many thoughts in your head."

As if they had been waiting for someone to break the ice, a chorus of voices chimed in after the old lady. But I was confused. *Thoughts? Is that why your hand turns into broccoli, because you have a lot on your mind?* I was about to ask the old lady with the grandson but someone called out Won-jun's name. "Ko Won-jun, the doctor's ready to see you." Raising his eyebrows, Won-jun got up and walked to the door. I leaned in to hear better, which proved unnecessary as the clinic was so small I could hear everything that was being said behind the door.

"Oh, broccoli! I haven't had a patient with this syndrome in some time. How long has this been going on?"

"I woke up this morning and found myself like this."

"That looks quite uncomfortable. Let's take a look, shall we? Does this hurt?"

"No."

"How about this?"

"That tickles."

"Tickles?"

"Yes. It tickles on the inside. I don't know what to call this, the stalk? Where my wrist should be? It tickles on the inside of that, underneath the skin. The vessels? Blood vessels? That's where it tickles."

"Oh, that's completely normal. Sounds like you're photosynthesizing. You know what photosynthesis is, right? I'm going to prescribe you some pills. Drink lots of water and get plenty of rest. That's what you need most. Try to relax and think peaceful thoughts. You'll be fine in a few days or so."

That was easy, I thought as Won-jun suddenly lowered his voice.

"Um... I..."

I was certain he'd asked a question but I couldn't hear what he was saying. What I only heard was the doctor's response.

"No worries, you'll get better in no time."

"...Thank you."

I heard the sound of a swivel chair pushing away. Won-jun walked out of the room, rubbing his broccoli arm with his left. He looked both annoyed and depressed.

We went to the pharmacy on the first floor of the building to fill his prescription. As soon as I got his meds, I opened the package to make him take one. It was a long, green, translucent pill. "It's to help remove the chlorophyll," explained the pharmacist, as I stood by the water dispenser, filling a glass half with cold water and the other half with hot water. With his left hand, Won-jun took the pill I offered him and popped it in his mouth. Watching his Adam's apple undulate as he swallowed the pill, I asked the question that had been bothering me.

"What's got you so stressed out that your hand turned into broccoli?"

Instead of answering, Won-jun gave me a long stare.

I remember having seen that expression somewhere before. Only after I had said goodbye to Won-jun and was walking to Pil-soon's house did I remember where I'd seen it. Once, when I was little, I had gone to the markets with Grandmother (not another patient but my literal grandmother on my father's side), where we bought a bag of peaches. When we got home and opened the bag, however, we saw that the peach on the top looked perfect but all the peaches on the bottom were covered in bruises. Angrily, Grandmother marched back to the fruit seller with the bag of peaches in one hand and me in the other. When she thrust the bag of bruised peaches in his face, the fruit seller gave her the same expression I had seen on Won-jun's face. Finally, he said, "But that's how it is with white peaches. White peaches bruise easily. That's just how they're built."

That's just how they're built.

That afternoon, Pil-soon, Gwang-suk, and I organized a simple funeral for Mal-ja. The venue was Pil-soon's front yard, although, since Pil-soon was renting the first-floor unit of the condo building, the front yard wasn't really hers. But we all agreed, even the landlord who lived in the same building, that the yard was the best place to bury Mal-ja. The landlord found a rusty old shovel from his shed for us to dig the grave. "My dog died last year. I buried her there, too," said the landlord, pointing at the shade of a yew tree, which made us even sadder and made the atmosphere more fitting for a funeral.

Mal-ja had always liked the color pink, so Pil-soon and I wore pink blouses while Gwang-suk wore a pink swim cap that he got from his swim club since he didn't have any pink clothes. We chose a wooden wine box to bury the bird in and placed several of her belongings inside, including her perch, some dried fruit, her toy ball, a wool bell, and five invoice statements for Pil-soon's gas bill. Mal-ja had always loved to tear those paper invoices into long, thin strips then parade around with the paper dangling from her tail. We arranged the items to make a small bed on which we placed the body of Mal-ja wrapped in the rose-patterned handkerchief. Then we closed the lid. His mouth firmly pursed, Gwang-suk grabbed the shovel and began digging below the spindle tree in one corner of the yard that he'd surveyed in advance. The earth was wet and soft so the digging couldn't have been that hard, but even so, Gwang-suk let out a low groan each time he struck the ground with the shovel. Pil-soon and I crouched down on either side of him and picked out the pebbles and pieces of twig that were mixed in with the dirt. When the hole became deep enough, we placed the wine box holding Mal-ja and covered it with loose earth. Then we patted it down.

Just like that, the funeral was over. It would have been a finer occasion had we read a eulogy of some kind but none of us had prepared anything. Besides, we were all covered in sweat from crouching in the sun for so long. I thought, *Sure would be nice to have a cold beer right about now.* Gwang-suk, looking like he was thinking the same thing, stood there with sweat lining his upper lip. But because Pil-soon remained in the yard, neither Gwang-suk nor I could find it in us to leave. Pil-soon was still stroking the earth, which was already flat and smooth. Rarely had she stroked the bird when it was alive or said one kind thing to her. All the curse words that Mal-ja hurled at people were picked up from Pil-soon herself. But neither Gwang-suk nor I saw fit to scold her with a, *Why weren't you nicer to Mal-ja when she was alive?* Instead we left her alone to stroke the earth to her heart's content.

Later, we trooped over to Pil-soon's apartment and washed our hands. Black dirt was caked under our fingernails so we used an old toothbrush to scrub each other's hands. I surrendered my hands to Pil-soon as I thought, *What a peaceful scene for a bunch of people who've just been to a funeral,* then looked up to see that the others were wearing the same look on their faces as we rubbed our hands dry on the towel.

I was supposed to be off the clock that evening—that is, I was originally hired to care for Pil-soon until 6 p.m., but that rule had flown out the window a long time ago. It was already very dark but I found myself still hanging out at Pil-soon's place. She began roasting some dried *jipo* fish fillets, so I eventually headed out to buy the beer I'd been craving all afternoon. Later, the subject of our conversation naturally came to Won-jun. When I remarked how concerned I was that Won-jun's hand had turned into a head of broccoli, Gwang-suk looked upset. After a long time silently gazing at the thin strips of dried fish, he murmured, "That poor kid must be going through a rough time."

"What rough time?"

Gwang-suk fell silent again and stared off into space. He opened his mouth, as if to say something, then heaved a heavy sigh instead. It was Pil-soon who eventually spoke up.

"When I was young, I came across some folks suffering from that terrible affliction. People would wake up one morning to find their finger had turned into a string bean or a red chili pepper. It turns out they were suffering on the inside. Maybe they were consumed with hate for someone else or with some other bad feeling. Letting bad thoughts sit in your mind for a long time will eventually break you down, you know. Turn you into something that's not human. The sick people got better after they ate some good food and rested for a few days, so we knew the disease wasn't fatal. But you just look silly the whole time you're sick and it inconveniences you something terrible. Awful affliction it is. I thought it was all but gone after they started vaccinating the kids. Won-jun must have gotten weak, poor child. Tell him to come over sometime. I'll boil some chicken for him."

Weak? I was about to laugh and remind her that Won-jun

was a professional boxer, when I suddenly felt a lump in my throat that made me shut my mouth. Physically, Won-jun might be stronger and healthier than anyone, but could I really say the same for his mental health? Thinking of how Won-jun had gazed at me so painfully the way the fruit seller with the bruised peach had, I let out a low sigh. What was haunting him so much to make his body react in that way? I may be a nurse but I knew nothing about what my own boyfriend was going through.

"I wonder what's causing him so much distress," I thought out loud, as I crushed my empty beer can flatter and flatter. Pil-soon didn't say anything. As we settled into silence, the TV continued to chatter away.

It was late by the time I set out from Pil-soon's place, when suddenly Gwang-suk stopped me. He whispered, "Will you and Won-jun set aside some time for me tomorrow?"

I turned and saw him peer intently into my eyes, his face made rosy pink either by his pink hat or the beer we had been drinking.

"Time?"

"Yes, time. I want to take you kids and Pil-soon to a mountain."

"Mountain? What mountain?"

"That's what sick people used to do back in my day. When you head into the hills and sing, you can cut down your sick days from ten to two."

"Sing? What do you mean?"

"Won-jun has to sing from the bottom of his lungs. Really belt one out. Then you'll see what I mean."

With that, Gwang-suk grabbed my hand and pressed it firmly, as if to compel me into joining him on his plan. His hand was so hot and wrinkled that I couldn't help but agree.

"Don't brush off what I'm telling you as the foolish talk of some old man, and tell your boy to meet me tomorrow, you hear?"

"Okay, okay."

Only then did Gwang-suk let go of my hand and slowly turn away. *Singing? Boiled chicken sounds like a much better idea*, I thought as I crossed Pil-soon's front yard. I didn't forget to take one last look at where Mal-ja lay before I pushed open the front gates. That loud parrot used to croak, "You leaving? Coming back soon?" each time I set out the door. The earth was still flat and smooth where she was buried, and a soft darkness had settled over the place as if a knowing hand had spread out a nice bed for her to lie in.

Gwang-suk would be giving Pil-soon a nice back rub right about now, probably whispering how he would bring her another pretty little bird to take the place of the dead one. He would tell her about tomorrow's plan to take a walk up the mountain with us. I stood before the front gates and looked up at Pil-soon's still-lit windows. After a while, I decided to head to Won-jun's house.

At first I thought no one was home, or at least I did when I pushed open the door to Won-jun's place. The house was completely dark but, more than that, there was a certain stillness over the place, like the feeling a house gives off when it's empty. But Won-jun's scruffy shoes that he would wear everywhere with the backs worn down like slippers were still by the front door. I called out, "Won-jun, are you in here?" before reaching down to remove my own shoes. Then I stopped. I could sense Won-jun was home. He was sprawled out on the sofa bed in the same position in which I'd last seen him. But in the dim light that filtered in through the window, I could see something wasn't right. It was more a feeling I had than anything I saw with my eyes. I knew the body on the bed belonged to Won-jun but somehow, it felt like he wasn't really there. It was as if someone had taken the different bits and pieces of him that I recognized and rearranged them to seem like the shape of Won-jun. Hesitating, I reached out to turn on the lights when suddenly, I heard his low, heavy voice.

"Don't turn on the lights. They're too bright."

I trained my eyes, now accustomed to the darkness, on Won-jun's broccoli arm. Just that morning, it was only his arm that was a broccoli stalk; now the green had spread to his shoulder and the florets had more than doubled in size.

"Did you take your meds?" I asked.

"No."

I felt a wave of anger at his nonchalant answer, but for some reason I couldn't bring myself to yell at him. Instead, I felt my heart sink as if it were being sucked down from below. I crumpled to the floor next to Won-jun. I breathed in the smell of newly-cut grass emanating from him. It was a fresh, green smell.

"Won-jun," I said.

"Yeah."

"Is something the matter?"

"No."

"Gwang-suk said this happened because you're going through something emotionally difficult.

"If something's bothering you, please tell me.

"Tell me.

"Please."

Won-jun lay there silently, as if asleep or dead. I felt like I was alone in the darkened room. I thought I might cry soon, but I was wrong. I was in fact already crying.

"Please tell me," I repeated.

Finally, Won-jun let out a low sigh. His breath smelled strongly of cut grass.

"I'll tell you, so don't cry."

Won-jun pulled his mouth to one corner and became lost in thought. I waited, dabbing at my eyes with the ends of my sleeve.

"To tell you the truth, I don't want to box anymore."

Won-jun drew in a deep breath then let it out just as deeply. Then he began slowly telling me his story, as if unraveling something tightly coiled from within his stomach.

". . . Do you know what the most important thing in boxing is? Focus. You have to focus on wanting to beat the other guy to a pulp. If your left hand isn't up to the task, you gotta use your right. If your right hand won't cut it, you gotta use your head. You have to *really* focus to knock the other guy out. To have that level of focus, you have to think details. You've heard of image training, right? You have to imagine the other guy bleeding and slowly losing his strength. You have to imagine him getting knocked down from your punches. Have you ever imagined something like that in your life? I'm sure you've met some people you don't like, but have you ever imagined beating someone almost to death, in really intricate detail?

"But you know what really sucks? I don't even hate the other guy! In fact, I like him! The other guys I'm up against in the ring, they've dedicated their lives to boxing just as much as I have and have built careers like mine. I want to be friends with these guys. And yet I'm standing there, imagining beating them to a pulp. After a while, I found it hard to throw those punches. I kept telling myself that this is only a match, that it's a sport, and that I'm doing my job, but, whether it be a sport or a profession, I still don't want to deal with pain. I don't like pain. I don't like feeling it and I don't like inflicting it. It sucks. And that's when I realized I don't want to box anymore. But of course, I couldn't throw my whole career away just like that. I didn't want to. Instead, I kept thinking and thinking about what to do. Then I came to a solution. I decided to start hating the other guy. I thought it might be easier to hit him if I came to hate him.

"But it wasn't easy to force myself to hate, just as it's impossible to force yourself to like something when you don't. I had to force the hate out of me. I came up with all kinds of reasons to hate the other guy and repeated them over and over in my head. *He's probably not as nice as I think he is. I'm sure he wants to beat me up, too. I have to knock him out before he knocks me out. I have to make sure he never comes crawling back to me again.* Even on my days off, I kept thinking these thoughts. I thought of all kinds of reasons to make me want to throw those punches, and to contain those bad thoughts inside my right-hand glove. Then one day, I woke up as broccoli."

With that, Won-jun threw a broccoli punch in the air. I saw the outline of the florets in the darkness.

"After this happened, I can't bring myself to feel angry at anything, as much as I try."

He jabbed the air a couple more times. Then he dropped his broccoli fist to his side.

"You're probably thinking I should give it up. You probably don't understand why I'm doing something that's causing me so much pain. But I've been boxing my whole life. This is the only thing I know to do—hating someone else. Hating them enough to punch them to a pulp."

With that, Won-jun went quiet. The room was left with nothing but darkness, silence, and the sad smell of cut grass. I opened my mouth to speak but nothing came out. I felt like I should say something, some words of comfort or of disapproval or *anything* after listening to such a long and difficult story, but after gulping at the air a few times like a fish out of water, all I managed to say was one word.

"Tomorrow."

Won-jun glanced at me. Even in the darkness, I knew there was no glimmer of hope in those dead, listless eyes.

"Gwang-suk suggested we go hiking tomorrow. He says you could . . . You could do a few things that are supposed to help you heal. We'll go tomorrow. Okay? We'll have a good night's sleep, and we'll all go hiking tomorrow."

Won-jun didn't respond. I reached out and felt around for his broccoli hand. Beneath the thick, warm stalk, I could feel the pulsing sensation of water coursing below the skin. The water will circulate around the head of broccoli then end up . . . where? Where exactly in Won-jun's body would it go?

I wondered. Would it go to the source of his hate and anger? If the hate comes into contact with pure, clean water, would it thin out as well? I stroked and caressed the broccoli stump for a long time. The insides of my stomach churned, as if my own hand was turning green.

It was noon the next day when Won-jun and I met Pil-soon and Gwang-suk near the entrance to the Mt. Gwanak hiking trail next to the main gates of the Seoul National University campus. The elderly couple were dressed in matching hiking clothes in bright, sunny tones.

We fussed over one another as soon as we met. I complimented the couple on their clothes and asked them where they had bought them, exclaiming over the pretty azalea color of their matching jackets while Gwang-suk grabbed Won-jun's left hand, the hand that hadn't turned into broccoli, and shook it up and down. "I've been meaning to see you, boy," said Gwang-suk as he grinned a big, satisfied grin while Won-jun said, "I'm Ko Won-jun," and smiled shyly as if he were embarrassed or maybe a little tired. Even so, Gwang-suk refused to let go of his hand and held on to it for a long time.

It was a weekday, but there were a good number of hikers on the trail and the four of us looked like a nice, happy family. The weather was clear and bright, making it perfect for a hike. Gwang-suk had scampered up and down this mountain all the time from a young age, and Pil-soon had often joined him on these walks, so naturally the two of them led the way with their long hiking sticks while the two of us fell behind.

Since we were still near the entrance of the trail, the surrounding scenery was more like a park and less a big forest, with people kicking up dust on the smooth, firm trail. Won-jun and I walked in the middle of the path, holding hands. While walking, I thought of what Won-jun had said last night. I've also had times when I felt intense hatred for someone or was forced to do things I didn't want to do, but the incidents somehow ended up working themselves out. At the time, I must have felt awful and angry, but soon the feelings went away on their own. The process might have taken some time or been quite complicated, but the feelings always went away in the end. Even the wildest of rages that built up inside me, that were so forceful that I'd bitten down on my lip and tasted blood and swore never to forget the injustice, eventually disappeared as if nothing had happened. And it wasn't like I actively tried to forget what happened. The incident that led to those feelings didn't itself disappear, but the bad feelings ultimately did. I could later look back on what happened and remember how I felt at the time. Some mechanism must have been working deep inside me to help me forget those bad feelings. Otherwise, I couldn't have become so numb to an anger that once felt so real. My body must have known that I wouldn't be able to function if I kept those feelings inside me for too long, so the mechanism in charge of bringing a sense of calm and order back into my life went into overdrive in those moments. Perhaps Won-jun had been trying to stomach too much pain and anger for far too long, to the point where his mechanism broke down. With nothing to filter out the hate and anger, he must have carried them in his body for too long, until one morning he woke up as broccoli man.

Once his arm heals, what should Won-jun do? I thought as I walked up and down the rolling hills. I was soon out of breath. Meanwhile, Won-jun was walking serenely, wearing the same tired, sleepy expression, while Gwang-suk and Pil-soon were already far ahead of us as two azalea-pink dots in the distance. I formed my two hands into a trumpet and shouted, "Gwang-suuuuuuk! Are we there yet?" At that, the two dots stopped and turned around and pointed to a spot some distance ahead as if to holler back, *Just a little further.* They must have been thinking of stopping somewhere midway up the mountain instead of climbing to the peak.

Thirty minutes later, we finally came across Gwang-suk and Pil-soon again, who were resting against a wooden fence. Pil-soon handed us an ice-cold bottle of water wrapped in a handkerchief. "You made it, you made it." Gwang-suk guffawed at the sight of me exhausted and barely keeping up.

"This place seems as good as any."

With that, Gwang-suk climbed over the fence and wandered out beyond the marked path. I hesitated, not knowing if we were allowed back there, but Pil-soon also climbed over the fence, followed by Won-jun. Left with no choice, I gingerly climbed the fence after them. Gwang-suk kept venturing further into the forest, brushing away the long grass. It wasn't clear whether he knew where he was going. The rest of us followed him down a steep path that grew increasingly steeper. Suddenly, the path came to an abrupt end at a sharp cliff. Looking down, I saw jagged rocks reaching up from the bottom of the cliff. One false move and we'd be done for. "It's dangerous over there, so don't get too close," said Gwang-suk as he reached into his bag to grab a rolled-up foil picnic blanket. He spread it over a wide, slightly bumpy rock, and we placed our bags on each of the four corners to weigh the blanket down. From her own bag, Pil-soon brought out several rolls of *gimbap* wrapped in foil, some drinks, and a Tupperware container holding fresh fruit. The food made for a nice picnic spread. We sat down and each grabbed a toothpick to use as forks.

"Before we start eating, we have to do what we came here for," Gwang-suk said. He stuck his toothpick into an apple slice and turned to Won-jun.

"Now, take off that towel and start singing."

"Sing? Here? Now?" Won-jun said, looking understandably confused.

"Don't give me that and belt one out!"

Won-jun glanced at me with a worried look on his face. I turned to look away, a smile working its way onto my lips. I felt bad for keeping him in the dark, but if I'd told him he had to sing, he would have never agreed to come along. Realizing what I'd done, Won-jun shot me a dirty look. But we were in the middle of a mountain. What was he going to do?

"Just give it a try," Gwang-suk suggested again.

"What song should I sing?" Won-jun wondered.

"Any song you want."

"But I don't know any songs."

"Then scream. Scream as loud as you can."

As Won-jun hesitated, I took off the towel wrapped around his broccoli arm. The broccoli looked even greener and fresher in the sunlight. Gazing at the broccoli, Pil-soon suddenly spoke up.

"Can I go first and shout something? I'm not going to sing."

"Sure, go right ahead," Gwang-suk said.

"Go ahead."

Pil-soon got up and carefully tiptoed to the edge of the cliff. About two steps away from the edge, she suddenly flopped to the ground, as if her head was spinning, and brought her hands to her lips. Inhaling deeply, she then let out a sharp yell.

"Mal-jaaaaaaaaaaaaaaaa!"

I expected to hear an echo, but perhaps because the forest was not deep enough, there was none. And yet Pil-soon sat there, continuing her yell.

"I didn't mean it when I said those horrible things to you! I didn't mean to hurt you!

"I hope you've gone to a good place!

"I'll see you soooooooooon!"

Pil-soon sat there for a while, staring off into the distance. Finally, she got up and dusted off the seat of her pants. Like a performer coming down from the stage, she returned to us with a shy smile on her lips. Gwang-suk and I greeted her with fierce applause. As Pil-soon sat down next to him, Gwang-suk gave her a big smile.

"Wow, that made *me* feel good!"

"Good job. Now it's your turn, Won-jun."

I thought Won-jun was going to wave us off but surprisingly, he stood up and coughed a few times. He looked at us each in turn before cautiously walking to the same spot where Pil-soon had been. What was he going to do? I stared at Won-jun, my heart pounding. Won-jun took one step further from where Pil-soon had sat. Bending down, he looked down below. I jerked upright. The thought suddenly came to me that he might jump. Just then, Won-jun let out a yell.

"AHHHHHHHHHHHHHHHH!"

It was an incredibly loud yell, at least ten times louder than Pil-soon's scream. Taken aback, the rest of us exchanged glances with each other. A flock of birds took flight from a grove of trees below the edge of the cliff. Ignoring them, Won-jun brought his hands to his hips, inhaled deeply, then launched into song.

"Until that day when the waters of the East Sea run dry and Mt. Baekdu is worn away!"

At his sudden outburst of song (or was it screaming?), the rest of us keeled over as if the wind had been knocked out of us. My goodness! So it was true he didn't know any songs! But he's singing the national anthem! Of all things! I laughed until my chest made strange hissing noises. Gwang-suk glared at me to keep quiet, but even he had tears in his eyes while Pil-soon was doubled over next to him, trembling with laughter. Ignoring the rest of us, Won-jun continued to sing the national anthem.

"God protect and preserve our nation! Long live our nation!"

"Good! Good!" Pil-soon shouted, as she clapped along to the song. I hollered, "Keep going, Won-jun! Louder!" Won-jun turned around and grinned. It was a grin beautiful enough to capture as a photograph, but also made me tear up for some reason. I was laughing so much that my stomach was getting itchy. Soon, Won-jun reached the end of the song. Clearing his throat, he walked back to us. I got up and gave him a hug. "Good job, good job," I murmured as I patted his butt, stroked his head, and even pinched his cheeks.

He downed a 500-ml bottle of water. "It's strange. All I did was shout a little, but I feel so much lighter," said Won-jun as he twisted his neck this way and that.

"I told you that would happen," smiled Gwang-suk. "You'll feel better in no time."

I didn't know how the yelling was supposed to heal Won-jun, but I for one felt great. In fact, I felt like I was going to burst into tears. It was just a little singing, just a little bit of shouting, but it made us feel so much better. It was like the feeling of switching from a thick, sweat-soaked winter comforter to a light and breezy spring blanket. I felt so much more relaxed. What was going on? Was it because we were deep in the mountains, surrounded by clear, cool air that sucked in all sound without giving off so much as an echo? I'd never heard Won-jun shout so loudly before. *I didn't think he had it in him*, I thought, breathing in the clear mountain air. *He can be so manly when he wants to be*. Suddenly, a piece of kiwi stuck to a toothpick appeared before my nose.

"Even the most majestic of vistas can wait til after we eat," Pil-soon said, smiling, as she handed me the toothpick. We were in the middle of Mt. Gwanak, surrounded by scenery that was not exactly majestic, but I ate what was given to me. The kiwi's tangy flavor made my mouth water and kept me wanting for more. Won-jun must have been just as hungry as he grabbed two pieces of *gimbap* with his left hand and tossed them into his mouth. I realized neither Won-jun nor I had eaten anything since yesterday. The *gimbap* soon disappeared but Pil-soon brought out plenty more food from her bag which I'd been regarding suspiciously because of how full it was: some fried tofu rolls, red bean jelly, popped rice, and even frozen barley tea for us to eat and drink and chew and swallow. The rice was a little warm and the fruit had turned slightly brown in some places but it was so delicious it brought tears to my eyes.

Just then, Won-jun stopped in the middle of chewing his fried tofu roll. Groaning, he frowned and turned to stare at his broccoli arm. Thinking he might have bitten a grain of sand, I turned to look at him.

"It's bursting," he groaned.

"Bursting? What's bursting?" I asked in alarm.

The rest of us gazed at his broccoli arm, with our toothpicks in the air. Won-jun kept groaning and grunting. Suddenly, he reached out and grabbed his greenish forearm.

"I can feel something bursting inside."

"Bursting?" I repeated.

"I don't know how to explain it. It feels like there are small fireworks going off inside my arm."

What? What does that mean? I was about to ask, feeling a growing sense of panic. Suddenly, Pil-soon and Gwang-suk began shouting and pointing at the same time. Gwang-suk grabbed Won-jun's broccoli arm and brought it close to his face.

"Look at this!" he yelled.

I brought my face close and saw what he was pointing to. There were small, yellow dots on his arm. One of the broccoli florets had grown taller than the others and was sprouting yellow dots on its tips. They were so tiny that we could only see them if we brought our faces close. But see them we could, and we instantly recognized what they were.

"Those are flowers, aren't they?" I asked.

"Well, broccoli are flowering plants . . . that have been cultivated to grow bigger heads . . ."

"Wait, you mean to say those small things are all flowers?"

We brought our faces closer to Won-jun's broccoli arm and spoke in hushed tones. Slowly but surely, tiny flowers were sprouting all over the broccoli tips. One of the first sprouts grew longer and longer until a tiny stalk emerged from the tip. From there, a bright yellow flower petal slowly wound its way upward and began to unfurl. Several minutes later, we saw the first fully blossomed flower. It was a tiny, simple flower with four petals forming a small cone. Soon, other flowers blossomed from the yellow tips.

"Oh, those are so pretty," Pil-soon exclaimed.

"Yes, they really are," I murmured.

"What a sight!"

We each murmured something in turn. I felt a wave of emotion come over me, as if I were seeing a newborn animal for the first time. I stroked Won-jun's shoulder.

"This feels weird," Won-jun said as he looked down at his broccoli arm. His face was much more at peace, his eyes and lips more relaxed.

"Yes, yes, you're all better now," Gwang-suk said with a pleased smile.

About an hour later, Won-jun's broccoli arm had turned into a big head full of flowers. Tiny flowers were adorning the head, with the flowers on the outermost tips drooping down while the flowers in the middle shooting up straight into the sky, altogether looking like a big, upside-down chandelier. When I held a flower between my fingers, it gave off a surprisingly strong peppery smell. It was a refreshing, very intense smell that was different from other flowers. We took turns carefully stroking the broccoli flowers, as if congratulating someone who had done himself proud. Each time our fingers brushed the flowers, they nodded and gave off their intense scent. It was a scent strong enough to last into our dreams.

The sweet and spicy smell would likely carry through the wind and head out far and wide, all the way to the entrance of the Mt. Gwanak trail, I thought with a sense of pride.

By the time we came back down the trail, the sun was setting. We went back the way we came and said our goodbyes in front of the campus gates. After sending an exhausted Gwang-suk and Pil-soon off in a taxi, Won-jun and I slowly walked to a fork in the road where we would have to say goodbye. Won-jun was carefully cradling his broccoli arm, still wrapped in a towel. He looked not unlike someone happily carrying a bouquet of flowers in honor of a joyous occasion. I walked home with a big bounce in my steps. I felt like bursting into song.

Since I had worked up a big sweat that day, I showered and climbed into bed as soon as I got home. I thought I'd fall asleep immediately given how tired I was, but when I lay down, sleep didn't come as soon as I thought it would. I was still excited from what happened that day, like a kid who had been to a picnic. Even though I closed my eyes, I could still picture the events of the day. I hugged my pillow close and tossed to my left, then to my right. I thought over what had happened.

I realized I was disappointed at Won-jun for not confiding in me sooner about wanting to quit boxing. He's usually so eager to talk about his thoughts and opinions, but when it came to sharing what he was feeling on the inside, he had kept me in the dark and suffered alone for all those months. *Couldn't he have told me how he felt?* I felt myself pouting in the dark. I guess I couldn't have offered him a solution even if he had told me. I might have attempted to cheer him up by offering to take him out to a nice restaurant or maybe go on a trip somewhere, like what Gwang-suk must have done for Pil-soon last night. I felt ashamed. I guess we're all the same when it comes to comforting the ones we love.

Would Gwang-suk offer to buy Pil-soon a new pet parrot? If he did, he was likely to buy a bird that was talkative and affectionate. The bird would be cute in a way that's different from Mal-ja, with a different voice and tone. But over time, it'd pick up curse words and start hurling them at random people, too. I was sure of it.

I felt sleep finally come over me.

The next morning, I woke up to find that Won-jun had sent me a text with an image attachment. *I decided to quit boxing*, he had written. The picture was of his right hand. There were still some flower buds near the tips that were withering away, and the hand was greenish in some places, but it looked like a proper human hand.

I typed back, *That's great!*

And it really was.

FINGERNAIL SHADOW

Late at night, I awoke to find Yong-jun staring down at me. Sleepily, I gazed up at the clock hanging on the wall behind him and saw that it was four in the morning, a reasonable time to be dreaming a bizarre dream. His piercing stare bothered me slightly, and the experience was rather scary and even a little tragic, but because this was a dream, I turned over in bed and was about to fall back asleep when I heard Yong-jun call out to me.

"Wake up, Soo-jung."

His voice sounded so much like Yong-jun's real voice, which I realize was a strange thing to say—obviously he sounded like Yong-jun because that's who he was, but it was odd to hear such a clear voice in a dream. I pulled up the covers and turned over to the side. As I did, I noticed Yong-jun's long legs.

"Wake up," he said again. Since he was speaking in that same familiar voice, with such an earnest expression on his face, I thought the least I could do was to oblige him. Giving up any attempts at sleep, I slowly sat up in bed. I saw the lights from the streetlamps outside the window shining across his sad face. *This must be real*, I thought. I had no choice but to think it was. The Yong-jun that was staring down at me felt more real than any memories I had of him.

"But Yong-jun, you're dead," I found myself saying. In fact, I believe I blurted it out. Yong-jun's expression darkened.

"Right. I am dead, aren't I."

With that, he fell into silence. I rubbed my forehead, feeling uncomfortable. Was I seeing a ghost? But I noticed the long shadow he cast behind him and smelled the familiar scent of Yong-jun in the air, along with the familiar smell of his clothes. His bearing and mannerisms were all eerily similar. *Maybe ghosts can give off a smell? Or maybe this is the smell of rotten flesh? But wait, I had Yong-jun cremated. I had him cremated then scattered his ashes somewhere near Yeongdo*, I thought.

"I'm a fingernail," came his voice.

"You're a what?"

Yong-jun fell silent again. He continued to stare down at me.

Next to me, a sleeping Suk-ki groaned and stirred.

"Who's there?"

Yong-jun and I answered simultaneously.

"He says he's a fingernail?" I said.

"I'm a fingernail," said Yong-jun.

"A fingernail?" Suk-ki yawned, rubbing his sleep-filled eyes. Sitting up, he looked at Yong-jun. Then he turned to me. He looked back and forth between the two of us, then spoke.

"Didn't you say this guy was dead?"

"Yeah, he is."

"So what's he doing here?"

"I don't know. Says he's a fingernail," I shrugged.

"A fingernail?"

Meanwhile, Yong-jun was scanning the bedroom, with its new flower-patterned duvet, the lotions lined up on the vanity, our small wastepaper bin and the clothes tossed over a chair. His eyes landed on a photograph hanging on a wall, and his expression turned to one of shock. It was Suk-ki's and my wedding portrait, taken last year. I had been the one to stubbornly insist on hanging that portrait in our bedroom ("This is what newlyweds are supposed to do!"), refusing to listen to Suk-ki, who had pointedly told me that I was being totally basic. Now, as I saw Yong-jun's pale face, I was filled with regret. Regret over what exactly, I didn't know, but the feeling was definitely one of regret.

"Are you married?" Yong-jun asked.

"Yes, I am," I replied.

"When did that happen?"

"Last year."

Then, because Yong-jun fell quiet, I didn't say anything, either. Yong-jun was dressed in his favorite khakis and the black short-sleeved shirt he loved along with a pair of clean white socks, while I was wearing a loose pair of pajamas with my hair all disheveled and unkempt. I was embarrassed. It had been so long since I'd seen Yong-jun. So long. But it would have been insensitive to try to make myself look more presentable, as it would be an affront to Suk-ki. Instead, I merely sat there, unsure what to do. Suk-ki and I remained sitting up in bed, with Yong-jun staring down at the both of us, when suddenly, Suk-ki leaped out of bed and turned on the overhead lights.

"What the hell is going on?" he yelled, with one hand still on the switch. I squeezed my eyes shut at the sudden flash of light, thinking that perhaps Yong-jun might be gone by the time I opened them again. Isn't that how ghosts behaved? But when I opened my eyes, Yong-jun remained standing there by our bed, still wearing his sad, pale expression. Standing there in the light, I noticed how Suk-ki and Yong-jun were of similar height and build, with the same facial expressions as well, to the point that they looked like they could be brothers. *Crazy how one's taste in men never changes*, I thought stupidly, scratching my forehead.

Dawn was breaking as we sat around the kitchen table. It felt awkward to just be sitting there doing nothing, so I decided to make some tea. Or perhaps coffee, since it was so early. Then I remembered how Yong-jun used to like the coffee I made for him. I made three cups and brought them to the table.

"Thank you," Yong-jun murmured, as he wrapped one hand around his mug, the other cupping it from the bottom. He sipped the coffee, making slurping noises as he did. He looked exactly as he had when he was alive, and, as far as I could tell, the coffee was coursing down his esophagus and making its way to his stomach instead of splashing to the floor. What exactly was going on?

"We need you to tell us exactly what is going on," Suk-ki said. Placing his mug on the table. Yong-jun became lost in thought. Suddenly, he looked up at me and asked, "When did I die?"

"It's coming on five years," I replied without missing a beat, which surprised me because I sounded like someone who had been keeping track all these years. The answer came almost automatically, as if I'd say the same thing if I were stopped in the street by a random stranger asking me the same question. It had been five years and two months. Upon hearing the answer, Yong-jun became lost in thought again.

"You don't recall your own death?" Suk-ki asked.

"No," Yong-jun said, "Although I'm aware that I'm dead."

"Do you remember how you died?"

"Yes, it was a bus crash."

Suk-ki glanced at me as if to ask, *Is that true?* I nodded. Yong-jun had been on a bus to his friend's wedding in Busan. The bus had slid in the rain and crashed into a guardrail, plunging down a steep cliff. Everyone on board died instantly. So did Yong-jun.

I had met the groom-to-be on several occasions before, so I was invited me to the wedding as well. But I didn't go. I had tried to cut my own bangs the day before and failed spectacularly.

I was also the reason Yong-jun had no choice but to take the bus rather than take the KTX speed train. Never a tech-savvy person, Yong-jun had asked me to book his train tickets for him, but it had completely slipped my mind. Only realizing this slip-up on the day of the trip, I hurriedly tried to book tickets on the KTX mobile app, but of course, there were no seats available. In the end, Yong-jun had to take the bus. The bus that slid and went belly-up in the rain. The bus that killed everyone on board.

Did Yong-jun resent me? For not being on the same bus? Or if I wasn't going to accompany him, the least I could have done was make sure he wouldn't have been on it in the first place.

How would I feel if I had been in his shoes? I would definitely be resentful. I am a resentful, cowardly person by nature. I would have been filled with resentment the instant the bus flipped over, the moment before I died, and even after my death. I would have vowed to come back as a ghost to take my revenge. What's more, if I had come back as a ghost and seen that Yong-jun had not only forgotten about me but had married someone else and was living the happy life of a newlywed? That would have been unforgivable. I would have done everything I could to avenge my death. I would have wrapped myself around his ankles as he walked down a flight of stairs, made him dream the same recurring nightmare of falling from an incredibly tall building every night, or indulged in other such petty acts of revenge.

Feeling sad and depressed at the thought, I stared down at my mug of coffee. Yong-jun spoke.

"I'm well aware that I'm dead. Although it happened so suddenly."

He continued in a low and calm tone.

"I remember being contained inside an unbearably cramped, dark place. My senses weren't intact, but I remember feeling cold for some reason. And it wasn't any kind of cold that I was used to from my life among the living. It was the kind of cold that came from inside my own body, not from the outside, if you get what I mean. I stayed in that cramped place for a long time like some ancient shadow. I wasn't necessarily trapped. I'm fairly certain I could have left and gone somewhere else if I had wanted to, but there was no place I wanted to be or anyone who was waiting for me. So I stayed there as a shadow. That's what I was. I merely remained there as a shadow, not doing anything, just lying there. Then suddenly, I thought of you, Soo-jung.

"And the instant that thought came to me, I couldn't stop thinking about you. There was no one else I wanted to see apart from you. I didn't have any other regrets about my life, and you were the only one I could think of. Time didn't exist where I was, so I don't know how long I remained in that position but I'm sure it must have been a long time. Then all of a sudden, my thoughts came to rest on… fingernails."

"Fingernails?"

"Yes, I used to bite my nails."

With that, Yong-jun shot me a meaningful look, as if to say, *You remember, right?* I wasn't sure what to do or say in return so I shrugged and hung my head. In fact, I wanted to tell him I remembered. Yong-jun liked to bite his nails, so much so that he never once in his life used a nail clipper. He would bite his nails down to the quick and didn't seem to be bothered at the sight of blood. Since he didn't give his nails any chance to grow, his nails were always a mess. He even had the disgusting habit of spitting out the nails around the house, which was such a jarring contrast to his otherwise neat and prim personality. I hated the feeling of stepping on his chewed-up fingernails so would place them on top of the desk or on the shelf each time I noticed them on the floor. The tangle of fingernail half moons resembled a heap of bones belonging to a small animal. I remembered this very clearly as if it were just yesterday.

"Did you ever hear that folktale of a fingernail transforming into a person?" Yong-jun asked.

"Didn't that story involve a mouse who ate the fingernail?" Suk-ki wondered.

"Really?"

"We don't have any mice here. We live in an apartment," Suk-ki said, in a rather stern voice. Yong-jun pursed his lips, looking uncomfortable.

"In any case, I imagined that I could turn into a fingernail. Then I thought that maybe your house might still hold some of my old fingernails, Soo-jung. And if that were the case, then maybe, I could come back to life by latching on to that nail. I mean, I had no idea how to go about doing it, but I thought and thought about latching on to the nail and then all of a sudden, *Whoosh*."

"*Whoosh*?"

"*Whoosh*. When I opened my eyes, I was standing here."

Yong-jun fell silent again. Suk-ki became lost in thought, his head resting in one hand. He was probably trying to decide whether what he had just heard was real or not, but I knew. I knew everything that Yong-jun said was the truth. Because the Yong-jun I knew was never one to lie, and that was what I loved about him.

"We were married last year," Suk-ki said, breaking the long silence. "We first met the year before, in July."

"I see," said Yong-jun.

"We don't have children yet, but we're planning to start a family soon."

"I see."

"I work at a company that imports paper and pulp, and, if things go well, I'll be promoted to a managerial position next year."

"I see."

"Soo-jung and I have had little arguments here and there but we haven't had a huge fight yet. We get along pretty well. For the most part."

"I see."

"So..."

"Yes?"

"So, would you mind leaving us alone?"

Suk-ki's voice was firm, leaving no room for argument. I remained quiet. What Suk-ki said was true. He was a good man and a good husband, and we were in love. It was impossible to say whether I loved him as much as I loved Yong-jun and whether such a thing could even be measured or compared, but if I were to be asked, point blank, whom I loved most in the world right now, I would say Suk-ki.

But I still couldn't bring myself to tell Yong-jun to leave. It was simply not something I could do, regardless of my love for Suk-ki. I'm sure Suk-ki knew this, which is why he decided to step up. For that, I was grateful and a little disappointed. I knew I shouldn't be feeling disappointed, but disappointment was what I felt.

"I tried to go back," Yong-jun murmured, rubbing the back of his neck with one hand. "I saw Soo-jung and saw you with her, so I thought it was best that I leave."

"I see."

"I felt relief at achieving what I'd come for. I don't resent anyone for what happened."

Yong-jun spoke in such a serene voice that I was on the verge of tears. He meant it when he said he wasn't resentful. But how could he not be? Was that even humanly possible? Or maybe it was possible now, since Yong-jun was no longer human.

"But I..." Yong-jun went on. "I don't know how to go back."

With that, he stared at the two of us with an inquiring look on his face, as if asking us for directions on how to return to the afterlife. But of course, neither of us knew how to go back. By this time, the sun had come up and was shining brightly on our familiar things—the potted plants and the couch and the laundry drying rack. As these items came into relief in the sunlight, the three of us remained sitting at the kitchen table, staring confusedly at one another.

It was time for Suk-ki to go to work. Yong-jun and I stood by the front door to see him off. Suk-ki said he would try to get the afternoon off if he could. The door closed behind him but I didn't hear his footsteps leave for a long time. Feeling guilty and hanging my head low, I peered at my shoes and Suk-ki's shoes by the foyer. Suddenly, I realized Yong-jun must not have any shoes. Not just shoes, but he wouldn't have any cash or a coat or a place to go. Yong-jun didn't have any family and he had very few close friends. That's why I was the only one he wanted to see and that's why he came here. My chest ached at the thought.

Meanwhile, Yong-jun had returned to the living room and was touching and admiring our things.

"Yong-jun?" I called to him. He turned around.

"Yes?"

"Did it hurt?" I asked, although that wasn't really the question I had in mind. Smiling, Yong-jun said, "No. It didn't hurt at all."

"How did it feel then?"

"It'd be more accurate to say I didn't have a chance to feel any pain."

"I see."

"But I was aware I was dying. I knew I was going to die."

"How did you feel?"

"Scared. I was very scared."

"Oh."

"I was willing to do anything if it meant I could stay alive. That's how scared I was," Yong-jun said, as he stroked the top of our new television. "To be honest, I was worried that you might have died, too."

"What do you mean?" I asked.

"Dying was such a scary, incredibly frightening experience. I worried that you might have gone through it, too. After death, there's nothing but a cold, cramped, and lonely place. I was worried you were stuck in the same place I was in."

"I don't understand..."

"What I mean to say is, I'm glad you're alive, Soo-jung."

I didn't know what to say, so I stayed quiet. I thought he might have been resentful that I hadn't died with him. I would certainly have felt that way. But Yong-jun went on admiring the television then turned to the weeping fig tree we kept in one corner. After a long while observing the plant, he grabbed some tissue and began gently wiping the leaves of the tree. I remembered how Yong-jun had loved to tend to his potted plants when he was alive.

"What do you typically do during this time of day?" he asked, still wiping the leaves.

"I clean the house then fix myself lunch. Sometimes I go out for groceries."

"I see."

"I don't have to go out for groceries today though. I went shopping yesterday."

"So what are you going to do now?"

"I'm going to fix myself something to eat. Are you hungry?"

The second I asked the question, I realized how silly it was. But Yong-jun responded casually, "No, I'm not hungry, but I'd like to try some of your cooking."

With that, he went back to tenderly wiping the dust off the leaves. Then, folding the tissue carefully into a square, he tossed it in the wastebasket. I usually fixed myself a piece of toast or had leftovers from the night before, but since I had a guest today, I felt I should prepare something a bit more grand. I wandered into the kitchen.

"What would you like?" I asked in the general direction of the living room while standing before the refrigerator.

"Anything," Yong-jun said, unhelpfully.

That's so typical of him, I thought to myself as I opened the fridge and studied the contents inside. There was nothing special, save for a lump of pork I was defrosting for tonight's dinner. I remembered we also had some aged kimchi I'd gotten from Suk-ki's mother. Deciding to make kimchi *jjigae*, I filled a pot with broth and turned on the stove. When I opened the lid of the kimchi container, Yong-jun called out, "Are you making kimchi *jjigae*?"

"Yes."

"It's been a while since I smelled kimchi." Yong-jun wandered over, sniffing the air, and peered into the container of kimchi. *Did he like kimchi?* I wondered. *If he did, what kind of kimchi did he prefer?* I knew that Suk-ki liked kimchi prepared without any pickled seafood, preferred the less fermented kimchi to the more aged versions, and enjoyed the leafy part of the cabbage rather than the stalks. But what about

Yong-jun? I must have known his kimchi preferences back in the day, but for the life of me I couldn't remember what they were. Feeling sad, I stood there as well, peering into the container. There was a time I'd prided myself on knowing everything there was to know about Yong-jun without having to be told—what his likes were, what he was afraid of, what he wanted—the way I know everything about Suk-ki today. But maybe I didn't know Suk-ki as well as I thought I did. If it were Suk-ki standing before me right now, instead of Yong-jun, I'd have thought the same thing. In that case, what exactly did I know, about anything? Maybe the only things I know are things about myself and myself only.

"The pot is boiling," Yong-jun pointed out. Pulling on a clear disposable glove, I grabbed some kimchi, sliced it with a knife, then tossed it into the pot. I folded in a spoonful of chili flakes and placed the pork inside as well. Just then, my phone rang. It was Suk-ki.

"Where is he?" Suk-ki asked as soon as I picked up.

"He's still here."

"What are you doing?"

"Cooking. *Jjigae*."

"Can he even eat?"

"I guess so?"

"I managed to get the afternoon off. I have a work lunch though, so I have to go to that first."

"Okay."

I could tell Suk-ki was about to say something more but, after a sharp intake of breath, he remained quiet. I stayed quiet as well, merely stirring the pot of *jjigae* while staring at the back of Yong-jun's head. From the other line, I could hear office background noise—the muffled sounds of conversation, the ringing of a phone, the sound of someone typing. Suk-ki must make those kinds of sounds as well during the course of his work day. They belonged to a world I wasn't familiar with. Just as Suk-ki wasn't familiar with the world I alone occupied after he left for work each morning.

"I have to go. I'll call again on the way."

"Okay."

When I hung up, Yong-jun turned to me.

"What'd he say?" he asked.

"He got the afternoon off. But he has to stop for lunch first."

"I see. He must be busy."

"Yes, he's been very busy lately. I think he mentioned a big project he's leading."

"Your husband sounds like a very competent man."

"He's a workaholic. He works all the time, even when he's home." As I said that, I felt my face flush with shame. I hadn't meant to talk behind my husband's back. Meanwhile, Yong-jun nonchalantly grabbed a pair of kitchen mittens off their hook and carefully lifted the pot of *jjigae* which he took to the kitchen table. He grabbed two bowls and, using our big wooden spoon, spooned some rice into the bowls. He also picked up two bigger bowls for the *jjigae*.

"We only have cold rice," I said apologetically.

"That's okay."

I wasn't hungry in the least but I sat at the kitchen table anyway. Lifting his spoon, Yong-jun said quietly, "*Bon appetit.*" Then he took a bite of the *jjigae*.

"It's good," he said.

Despite what he said, I wondered whether the food really was good. I spooned some *jjigae* over my rice, stirred the bowl, and had a bite. I was furiously chewing the rice which felt like beads of plastic, when Yong-jun asked, "How did you and your husband meet?"

"My friend introduced him to me. Remember Eugene?"

"I remember, the tall friend."

"Yes, they went to the same school."

"That's great."

"Yes."

"Tell me more. I'm curious."

"There's nothing more to tell. It's a boring story."

"Still, I'd like to know."

It wasn't like Yong-jun to be so persistent. With my wooden chopsticks mid-air, I wondered what to tell him.

"Well, the first time we met, it was in a Japanese *izakaya* in Hapjeong. I had heard he wasn't much of a drinker but he insisted we meet at a bar. I didn't have any expectations going into the date but both of us ended up drunk that night. He told me later he'd gotten himself drunk because he was so nervous."

"Mm-hmm."

"I didn't hear from him for a few days after that, so I assumed things hadn't worked out. But later, he called and asked me out again, but this time, he insisted we should both stay sober. So we met and watched a movie, but after that, there was nothing for us to do, so we went back to a bar. And we ended up getting drunk again."

"That's funny."

"What's really funny is that we met five times and all five times, we ended up getting super drunk. He's such a shy guy that he ended up proposing only after the sixth date. Since neither of us was getting any younger, we decided to get married straightaway."

"And for your honeymoon? Where did you go?"

"The Maldives. It was a nice place, with nice weather, nice scenery, nice people, everything was nice."

"You got your wish then. You always wanted to go to the Maldives."

That was true. I had mentioned to Yong-jun that I wanted to go to the Maldives for my honeymoon. Yong-jun had agreed, then asked what currency they use in the Maldives. We had looked it up online. Did I think of Yong-jun while honeymooning in the Maldives with Suk-ki? Did I think of him as I took out crumpled bills of *rupiyaa* from my pocket to pay for mango juice and spicy crab? No, I didn't. I hadn't thought of him at all. What I did think about was how great the weather was and how pretty the beach was. I was only preoccupied with how happy I was.

"I'm sorry," I said.

"For what?"

"I forgot we had planned to go there together."

"Why would you feel sorry for that? I'm the one who died."

"But you didn't want to die."

"And you didn't want to forget."

I didn't know what to say to that.

Yong-jun said, "May I ask you a question?"

"You can ask me two."

"How were you after I died, and before you met your current husband?"

I looked up and saw Yong-jun pretending to chew his food while pointedly staring away from me. I knew what he wanted to hear but didn't want to give him the satisfaction.

Sullenly, I said, "Of course I was sad. I was sad."

"You were?"

"Of course. I had to arrange your funeral and take care of your things. I had you cremated, with the ashes scattered over the seas of Yeongdo. You told me your family is from there."

"Right. Thank you for everything."

"You sound like you were looking for a different answer."

"You're right."

"You want to know how sad I was, and how I expressed that sadness."

"That's right."

I resented him for admitting to it so breezily, but since he asked, I decided to tell him.

"I cried the whole time," I continued. "I regretted everything. If only I had remembered to buy those train tickets for you online. If only you had taken the plane instead of the bus. If only I had told you to take the economy bus instead of priority class. I cried so much my tear ducts became inflamed and I had to visit the hospital. I lost a lot of weight."

"Really?"

"Yes. After crying myself to sleep, I saw you in my dreams. I was so angry because instead of resenting me for basically killing you, you looked so happy and peaceful, like in the old days. Together, we shared meals and went for walks. Then I'd wake up and realize you were gone. I didn't even have any photos of you since you hated getting your picture taken."

"I'm sorry. Want to take a picture of me now?"

"No."

"What happened after that?"

"What else? Just life."

"What do you mean, 'life'?"

Meanwhile, Yong-jun had finished his rice. He tucked the empty rice bowl inside the empty soup bowl then placed his spoon and chopsticks over the bowls. Getting to his feet, he took the bowls and utensils to the sink and ran water over them. *How thoughtful of him*, I thought as I placed my half-finished bowl of rice inside the sink as well.

"Life happened. I thought I'd never forget you and I believed I shouldn't forget you, but forget you I did."

"You forgot about me."

"It didn't happen overnight. It was gradual. Like, imagine if you were a teacup that had shattered into a thousand pieces. At first, I made sure to keep every little bit of you, down to the tiniest grains of shattered glass. But then, the little bits became lost. Soon, I was left with only the bigger pieces. The pieces used to be so sharp that they'd cut my hand when I picked them up but over time, they became rounder and duller."

"I know what you mean."

"You can be angry at me if you want."

"I'm not angry at you."

"But you must be. You're right to be angry at me. I promised I'd never forget you, that I'd love you forever, and now…"

"Were you angry at me when I died?"

"Yes. But the anger soon ebbed away. I just wanted to see you again."

"I feel the same way. And one day, if I can continue to exist somewhere, in some form, I'll come to forget you, too."

Yong-jun returned to his seat. He grabbed some kitchen wipes and wiped a few spots of spilled stew on the kitchen table. I bit down on my lips and held back my tears as I saw his fingers clutching the wipes. The effort crumpled my forehead and made me pout but I still fought them back. I willed myself not to cry and knew that if I did I would regret it the rest of my life.

"That's how it is," Yong-jun whispered softly.

Suk-ki returned around two in the afternoon. As soon as he walked in, he asked calmly if we'd eaten. I said we had, knowing that he had asked me the same thing over the phone. Yong-jun got up awkwardly from his seat on the sofa and nodded in acknowledgment, and Suk-ki nodded back. Unsure what to do, the three of us ended up in the same formation we'd made that morning, sitting around the kitchen table.

Clearing his throat, Suk-ki began, "I've been thinking. I think you might not have fully come to terms with the fact that you're dead."

"What do you mean?" Yong-jun asked.

"Well, most dead people disappear. They don't linger anywhere."

"Hm."

"But you said you felt like you existed as a shadow in a dark, narrow place somewhere."

"Yes."

"Maybe that's because you couldn't accept the fact that you're dead."

"Maybe."

"While at work, I looked up news articles of your accident. Of your death. The articles all said that everyone in the bus—I'm sorry to say—died instantly."

"Yes, I believe we did. At least, that's how I remember it."

"Yes. In your head, you know you're dead but you still haven't come to terms with it, if you get what I mean. That's why you stayed back in this world and attached yourself to a piece of your fingernail. No offense."

"None taken."

"So I think that maybe we should head over there."

"Head over where?"

"To the site of the accident. The articles said that it occurred somewhere near the Chungju Interchange. Maybe if you see the actual site, you might feel differently. At least, that's the idea I had."

The idea was very typical of Suk-ki. Privately, I didn't think it would work. I didn't have any claims to the contrary, nor did I have any alternative ideas to offer. But I didn't think his idea would work. When I glanced at Yong-jun however, he had a thoughtful expression on his face.

Nodding, he said, "That's a good idea."

"Okay then," Suk-ki said. "Let's leave right away."

Getting up from his seat, Suk-ki grabbed the jacket he had slung over his chair. Since they'd made the decision to head out, I hurriedly changed into something more appropriate to wear outside and pulled a cap over my head as I didn't have time for a shower. We were just about to head out the door when Suk-ki hesitated before the foyer.

"What is it?" Yong-jun asked.

"Shoes. You don't have any shoes."

"Oh, right."

As Yong-jun stood there, unsure what to do, Suk-ki threw open our shoe closet. Reaching deep inside, he grabbed a pair of rubber slippers and placed them by the front door.

"Here you go. You can take them with you if you want."

"Thank you."

Take them with him where? I thought to myself, smiling. The slippers were a perfect fit for Yong-jun's feet, and I was pleased at the realization that the two men did indeed share a similar physique and build. We took the elevator down to the sub-level parking lot. Suk-ki and I rode in the front while Yong-jun sat in the backseat.

"This is a nice car," Yong-jun remarked, taking in the car's interior.

"Buckle up," Suk-ki said, to no one in particular. Absentmindedly, I tugged at my seatbelt and buckled myself in. Suddenly, Yong-jun started laughing.

"I guess I don't have to wear mine," he choked between stifled laughter.

Suk-ki glared at him through the rearview mirror, but I thought I could detect a hint of a smile playing on his lips. But instead of breaking into a full smile, Suk-ki turned on the GPS and typed in "Chungju IC" into the system. "One hour, fifteen minutes to destination," the voice on the GPS announced merrily. *Does that mean Yong-jun will disappear in an hour and fifteen minutes?* I wondered, as the car took off.

Suk-ki focused on the road, his lips tightly pursed. We soon merged onto the freeway. I glimpsed at Yong-jun in the backseat. He was looking out the window at the paintings on the soundproof walls mounted on both sides of the freeway, wearing an expression of utmost serenity. He didn't look like someone who was going to disappear anytime soon, but I wasn't sure. I turned to face the front and sat quietly until we reached our destination.

"I think this is it," Yong-jun said. We parked our car on the shoulder and got out. We had overshot the interchange by a few meters and were standing by the side of the freeway, buzzing with cars hurtling past at breakneck speed. There was an overpass high above us, so high that we'd have died instantly if we'd been thrown off the edge.

The freeway shoulder where we'd parked was paved with pebbles and had clumps of grass growing here and there, along with a few sprays of cone flowers. Next to us stood a sign warning of falling rocks. A single line of white paint separated the shoulder from the road. There was nothing to hint at the deaths of all those people so many years ago. In fact, the place seemed downright cozy. Suk-ki must have had the same thought. With his hand on his forehead to shield his face from the sun, he looked out across where we stood.

"Yes, this is it. It happened right here," Yong-jun said over his shoulder after taking a few paces into the grass. As the accident had occurred five years ago, there was nothing there save for knee-high grass and a few bugs scared into scattering high in the air.

"I know this must be hard, but please try to remember," Suk-ki said.

"I'll try."

With that, Yong-jun crouched down on the patch of grass where he had stood and closed his eyes. I couldn't tell if he expected anything to happen but I remained quiet, watching him. The afternoon sun blazed down on our three heads. Many-winged bugs clung to our arms. The smell of fresh, trampled grass lingered in the air. It occurred to me that we may have looked like we were enjoying a picnic.

Just then, Yong-jun disappeared.

Suk-ki and I both yelled out in alarm and ran a few steps to where he had been. Where Yong-jun had been mere seconds ago, there was nothing but a pair of Suk-ki's old, three-striped slippers. He was gone. We had been staring at him, intently staring at him, when suddenly he had vanished without a trace. Shocked and flustered, I stood there not knowing what to do. Suk-ki went near and stooped to pick something off from one of the slippers. He then placed it on his palm and stretched it out towards me.

"Look."

I knew what it was even before I'd looked. It was an old, yellowed wedge of fingernail. I picked up the dried up, curled up piece of nail from Suk-ki's palm and stared at it. It really was a fingernail. When I pinched down on the fingernail with my thumb and forefinger, it struggled for a bit then broke into two. With the tip of my shoe, I dug a small hole in the earth and buried the fingernail pieces inside. Suk-ki, after watching this entire ritual in silence, finally spoke.

"Let's go."

"Okay."

I turned to grab the pair of slippers Yong-jun had left behind, but thought better of it, knowing that Suk-ki would never wear them again. We returned to our car and Suk-ki set the GPS to find our way home. When he turned on the AC, cold air blew from the vents. Only then did I realize how warm I was.

"That was really strange," Suk-ki said, his hands clutching the steering wheel.

"Yes, it was," I agreed. Suk-ki pulled out of the shoulder and took a left to join the freeway. Now that everything was over, I felt an odd sense of relief. Coupled with the fact I had been up since before dawn, I could feel sleep coming over me. I hung my head and closed my eyes, and as I did so, Suk-ki gently accelerated the car. I glimpsed at the side mirror and saw the shoulder growing ever more distant. *Goodbye*, I thought.

I hadn't mentioned this to either Yong-jun or Suk-ki, but I had been to the site of the accident before. I had visited less than a year after Yong-jun's death. I wasn't able to pinpoint the exact location where the accident happened, but I found a spot I thought was close enough. There I sat. Although I couldn't detect any trace of Yong-jun, I remained sitting there for a long time, increasingly becoming coated with grime from the passing traffic. I meant to die there. Either I was going to throw myself in front of an oncoming vehicle or slash my wrist. Either way, I was going to die right there. That way, I could be reunited with Yong-jun. The likelihood of meeting him would increase if I died at the same spot, or so I reasoned. That's why I had gone to that site. That's why I waited.

I don't know why I didn't follow through on the plan. In fact, I don't even recall how I got home. What happened? It must have been an insignificant reason that brought me home. Maybe I suddenly had a craving for a Coke or wanted to know how my favorite TV series would end. Yes, it must have been something trivial. Something impossibly inconsequential.

Sitting in the car, I felt a sensation of being pulled forward, as if something were struggling to push out from inside of me from somewhere near my back and pelvis. It was such a sudden and such a real feeling that I felt a physical emptiness in my stomach after it happened. When I turned around, I saw a long black shadow forming behind me, growing increasingly longer. I couldn't see where it ended, but I thought I could take a good guess.

The car kept racing on and the shadow kept growing longer and longer and thinner and thinner until suddenly, it broke off. When it did, I felt my body jerk a little but I wasn't surprised. I didn't even look back. I remained in the passenger seat, my body seated low, and gave in to sleep. As I did, Suk-ki backtracked the way we came and took us home.

THE GREY HERON CLUB

Yang-mi's Banchan officially went out of business last month on the tenth. The exact date was debatable depending on one's definition of "going out of business." In fact, it was much earlier than last month when I first started to notice I wasn't getting as many customers as before and that my little deli's expenses had surpassed its income. Clearly, it was much earlier than last month when things started going downhill. In any case, it was on the tenth of last month that I filed for business closure, so that day would be recorded as the day my shop officially went out of business. I, Yang Yang-mi, am a committed diarist, meaning I'm serious about recording my daily experiences the day they occurred, whether they were good or bad. The diary entry for the day I filed for closure consisted of a single sentence written in red ink for some bizarre, terrible coincidence. "File documents to close business: Gwanak-gu district website." This was less a journal entry than a to-do note to myself, but journals are meant to record the day's events and nothing captured the most significant event of that day than that single sentence. I believed it would suffice. After writing in my diary, I went to the website of the Gwanak-gu district office and filed for closure of my small business. Then I was at a loss for what to do. I had nothing to do and nothing I wanted to do. Just because my business was over didn't necessarily mean that my life was, but I suddenly lost all interest in anything I had ever known before, as if in closing my business I had pulled down the shutters on my life. Still, the day was much too long to be doing nothing. So I decided to walk. I walked as if it had been my sole purpose in life to walk, as if I'd been meaning to walk as soon as I'd shut down my business, as if I'd intentionally run my business to the ground so I could take to the road. I walked from early morning to dusk, doggedly and desperately.

At first, I spent the day walking down the streets. The Sillim subway station lay just twenty minutes away, and, the surrounding area being a busy district, the place was populated with shopping malls, used bookstores, and cafés. There was much to see and peruse, so I began going there. Not wanting to spend money on frivolous things, especially since I was out of work, I didn't buy anything. I simply window-shopped and touched and stroked the items in the shops as much as I could without drawing too much attention to myself. I stood in bookstores reading or headed to the movie theater to see what the latest offerings were. But soon I grew weary of being in crowded places full of people and I hit a limit looking at things I had no intention of buying. Because the area around the subway station was so busy, there were new businesses opening up every day and others closing just as often. It broke my heart to see that. I would stand in front of yet another shuttered business, staring blankly inside the darkened window. After too many times doing this, I found it difficult even walking by any shop or small storefront.

So I headed to the Dorimcheon Stream. Dorimcheon wasn't much of a sight to behold, being a narrow, shallow river, but it was lined on one side with a long walkway paved with soft polyurethane foam, while the other side of the river was adjacent to a bike path. Both the walkway and the bike path stretched as far as the eye could see, almost as if one could walk forever on them. The only thing you needed was a pair of strong, working legs. Without having to worry about where I was headed or where I wanted to go, I simply walked and walked in a dull, repetitive fashion, like a wind-up tin robot. It was early summer so the weather wasn't overbearingly hot. Still, I became drenched in sweat after many hours on the path and saw that I'd passed the Sindorim subway station, Anyangcheon Stream, and numerous signs announcing the number of kilometers left to the Han River, until I realized I could very well walk to the Han River as long as I stayed on this path. I might have gone there if I wanted to, but I never once made the trip. The Han seemed like one of those places where one would go to have fun, a place full of joy and light. Whereas right now, I was not in a situation to go to such a place. When I felt myself drawing nearer to the Han River, I turned around and headed back the way I came. Even as my body was in walking motion, I was no longer conscious of the fact I was walking.

As I walked, my thoughts wandered to how I had lost the business.

When I first opened the *banchan* deli, I made pretty good revenue. The store was located near a college campus on a small alleyway crowded with studio apartment buildings. The low rent was one appealing factor, but what attracted me to that spot was that the area was filled with young singles. My expectations proved correct. During the day, college students dropped by to buy plastic packs of fried spam, spicy pork stir-fry, and chopped hot dogs, while in the evening, young working professionals bought pickled cockle shellfish or fried kimchi cakes to enjoy with a beer. Often, I'd run out of the more popular *banchan* before the day ended. I also printed loyalty cards the size of business cards which were stamped with every purchase. Customers who managed to save ten stamps got a free *banchan* pack. There were customers who came in to redeem their card after just three days. "Well? What do you think?" "How's the food?" "Do you like it?" I wasn't shy about asking my regular customers what they thought of the food, and, unsurprisingly, most of them told me the food was great. Relieved, I worked all day, happily. Even as I washed the spinach and boiled the cuttlefish and chopped up the green onions, standing in the kitchen all day, taking in the variety of smells and having my face blasted with hot steam, I never grew tired of the work. After I'd packaged the *banchan* into their disposable plastic packs then stacked them in neat little rows, I felt as pleased as if I'd stacked a tidy pile of gold bricks.

It was about six months in that I first noticed something was off. Typically, I took home the *banchan* that hadn't sold that day and ate them for dinner. One day, I realized that I was bringing home packs of *banchan* that would normally sell out during the day. These were *banchan* such as pork stir-fry, egg rolls, and pork kimchi stew—all reliable bestsellers. At first, I didn't think much of it. But when the same thing happened every day for a week, then nearly two weeks, even I began to suspect something was wrong, which was saying a lot as I wasn't the sharpest when it came to picking up signs. One evening, as I sat at my table chewing the leftover *banchan* that felt like grains of sand between my teeth, I pushed the plates away and stood up. I grabbed my book of transaction records and receipts and attempted to make a full settlement of accounts, which I hadn't done once as I had been too busy. Immediately, I saw that profits were falling, noticeably.

After that, the climb down became steeper. I did my best to cook delicious *banchan*, with the nutty, flavorful aroma of sesame oil wafting from my deli, but no customers came. I put up a sign outside the shop advertising the day's special. I announced a 2+1 deal where anyone who bought two packs of *banchan* could take one more for free. But it was no use. I hired a kid to pass out flyers and stayed up nights posting online ads on websites for locals in the area. Nothing worked.

I still had a few straggling customers come in the evening but even they petered out. I sat in the cashier's chair, gazing out blankly at the empty store. As the *banchan* kept in the refrigerated display case grew steadily colder, so did my body. As I sat there waiting for customers that didn't come, my body grew colder and colder to the point I lost all warmth and felt the last breaths escaping me. It was then that I was swept with the feeling of betrayal. I was overwhelmed by a sense of injustice, as if the entire town had gathered together and swore never to go to my deli again and I was left out of the joke. Stuffing the leftover *banchan* in my mouth, I cried furious tears and yelled at no one in particular, wondering why the food wasn't selling when clearly it tasted good. Several months passed. I still had rent to pay, and, although I had no customers, I still had to pack the *banchan* into the packs. Basically, I was pouring money into resuscitating a dying business.

Then, one day, after yet another uneventful morning, a solitary customer walked in late in the afternoon. Watching her opening and closing the doors to the refrigerated display, I blurted out, "Why do you think the *banchan* isn't selling?"

The customer turned to me and dug her earphones out of her ears. "Excuse me?" she asked. I was already regretting having blurted out the question, but since I'd said what I'd said, I decided to follow through. I repeated the question to her. Frowning, she stammered for a few seconds then said, "Well… I guess it's because there's other food out there that's tastier than *banchan*."

She followed that up by insisting that she didn't mean that *my* food tasted bad but the damage was done. She placed the packs of tossed woodfern and zucchini cakes back where they belonged after taking forever to pick them out in the first place, then left the store. I didn't blame her. I'd have done the same thing if the store's owner asked me that question, but I still couldn't help feeling bitter. That evening, I closed up shop early. Leaving the *banchan* in the display, I came home and sat in front of the TV, which I normally don't even watch. That was when I realized for the first time that I could very well go out of business.

But the realization didn't lead to anything. I might have entertained the notion that I could go out of business, but I still didn't consider it to be a real, actual possibility. So I spent the next few months again wasting money and time and labor. In fact, even after I had made the decision to actually close the business, and even as I was handing over the cooking supplies and equipment to a used goods dealer, I still didn't grasp what was happening. The next morning, when I woke up but realized I had nowhere to go, I lay there rubbing my face into my pillow, still unable to believe what was happening.

While walking the length of Dorimcheon, I realized this was the reason I had gone out of business. I had no sense of reality, always defaulting to hopeless optimism and believing without any merit that everything was going to be okay.

Of course, that wasn't the only reason why I failed. When I started thinking of the reasons, I saw there was no end to them and that each reason was a perfectly sound, standalone reason for why I'd failed. Of all the businesses I could have possibly gone into, I had decided to sell *banchan*, which, like that customer had said, wasn't the most delicious thing on Earth. I had refused, out of principle, to add any artificial flavorings to my *banchan*, believing that this was the healthier option. I hadn't taken out advertising on the side of the local buses, thinking the costs would outweigh the benefits. Each time I thought of a new reason, I recorded it in my diary. At night, I sat and read over the reasons, hating myself with each read. After many days of walking dozens of kilometers every single day, I stopped walking. I still headed down to Dorimcheon each morning as if by force of habit, but, after a brief walk, I sat on one of the many benches or on a large, flat rock and stared off into the distance. There I would sit for the entire day, after which I'd return home.

Then one day, as I was sitting at a bench staring at the stream, someone came and sat next to me. I was lost in my own thoughts of anger and resentment and didn't even notice. The person sat there as I did, and stared off into the distance instead of peering into her phone or reading a book. Suddenly, she spoke.

"You come here often."

Surprised, I turned to face her and saw that she was a woman around my age. I looked her up and down. I did come here often but she didn't look familiar. I was in no mood to study the people I passed during my walks, and I imagined this woman must have a suspicious reason to speak to some rando on the street. I turned away. The woman remained seated there, looking off into the distance with a twinkle in her eye. Curious as to what she was looking at, I followed her gaze and saw a tall grey heron standing on the banks of the river near a thicket of dead reeds and grass.

"Watch closely. I think she'll make it," the woman said, without taking her eyes off the bird. Not sure what she was talking about, I found myself staring at the grey heron as well, wondering if I'd ever noticed a bird that big in these parts. Just then, the heron stabbed at the water with its long beak. In that instant, the stranger and I both let out a loud gasp. When the heron came back up, we saw a gleaming silvery minnow thrashing in the bird's beak. The heron tossed back its head and swallowed the fish in one gulp then walked away in the most nonchalant manner.

"Wow, she's really good," I murmured softly, my hands clasped tightly together. The woman smiled.

"Right? It's so much fun to watch them!"

I wouldn't call it so much fun as just slightly interesting. Not wanting to have her control this chance encounter we were in, I forced myself to revert to my stony expression. Ever since I'd lost my business, I'd been wearing what felt like a slab of cracked stone as my face, so it was easy to default back to this stony expression. As I did so, I realized there had been a hint of a smile playing at my lips. Why had I smiled?

Because some bird caught a fish? What an idiot. I'm sitting here grinning like a fool over some river fowl after I'd lost my business. As if she'd been reading my thoughts, the woman spoke again.

"See? Isn't it funny how one smile leads to another?"

Unnerved, I stared at the woman. *You don't even know me to say that about me*, I was about to shout at her, but I kept my mouth shut, thinking it was probably best not to engage her at all. Just as I was about to get up from my seat, the woman looked up at me and asked, "Would you be interested in watching more grey herons?"

What was she talking about? I was about to yell at her in a fury when the woman raised a finger to her lips and nodded at the grey heron. Almost automatically, I turned and caught sight of the bird just as it dipped its beak into the water again. The movement was precise and efficient. Again, it came back up with a fat minnow in its mouth which it swallowed whole.

"It sure is a sight," I murmured to myself without realizing what I was saying. The woman smiled proudly at me.

After I'd sat back down on the bench, I learned from the woman that her name was Kim Ha-young and that she came to this river every other weekend to watch grey herons. In fact, there were two other women in this bird-watching group, giving it the sense of being an official club of sorts. I smirked at how committed they were to something so silly and also at how this stranger was trying to have me join the club. But it was too late to back out of it now. I typed my number into Ha-young's phone, not sure whether I was doing the right thing.

"Would the other members be okay with me joining you guys?" I asked, not because I really wanted to know but out of a sense of courtesy, and really, as a way to hint at her that I didn't want to join at all. Ha-young waved her hand and shot back confidently, "Don't you worry. They were all open to the idea. In fact, they told me to make sure to land you as a member."

Then she added, "To be honest, I'd been watching you the last few days. I mean, I didn't mean to, but you were so conspicuous."

"Me? I'm conspicuous?"

At that, Ha-young's eyes widened in surprise. "Course you are! You must not pay any attention to your surroundings. Look around you. Look at all the people strolling happily on this weekday afternoon in the warm sunshine, drinking in all this clean air. No one else looks the way you do."

I was at a loss for words.

When I looked around, I saw she was right. In the pleasant, buzzy warmth of early summer, everything—from the skies to the trees—was clear and bright. Dandelions shone brilliantly like gold coins in the shrubs lining the walkways. Willow trees hung lazily over the river which flowed merrily, sunlight streaked across the surface like ribbons of silver. And the people who were drinking in these surroundings, these beautiful surroundings, people out with their dogs, lovers sharing ear buds, joggers focused on their laps, friends enjoying hot dogs—they were of various ages and appearances, but their faces all wore a soft, relaxed expression. I was the only drab individual amidst all this glorious beauty, I realized. I was the only one dark and depressed enough to have stood out among the crowd. When I realized this, I felt something heavy and hard press down somewhere on my chest.

"It's okay," Ha-young said calmly. "We all have times like those."

With that, she patted me on the shoulder as if we were longtime friends. Surprised by this behavior, I retreated into myself.

"We're going to meet this Sunday so if you're interested, come meet us. I'll text you when and where."

Ha-young stood up. Using one hand to shield her face from the sun, she squinted out at the river to where the grey heron had flown off. She must be going to find the bird.

"Well, I'm off."

Ha-young began walking upstream. Dazed, I looked after her and saw her leave. She was quite tall with a pair of very skinny legs, not unlike the grey heron we'd just seen. *Maybe she's one of them?* I thought bizarrely, then shook my head. *No wonder you lost your business*, a voice said from inside my head. *You always think the stupidest thoughts.*

On two o'clock that Sunday afternoon, I found myself standing by the entrance to the Sillim Theater, pressing the toes of my sneakers into the ground. I was debating whether this was a good idea or not. In fact, if Ha-young hadn't spotted me first and come running up to me with a hearty "Hey, Yang-mi!" I would have turned around and left.

"I didn't think you'd come," she smiled. Behind her were two women who were slowly bringing up the rear. One looked to be in her early fifties while the other must have been a college student, probably a freshman or sophomore.

The younger girl had a thick leather strap around her neck at the end of which hung a digital camera the size of her palm.

"Why don't we do the introductions later? First, let's find those grey herons."

After we'd awkwardly nodded at each other, Ha-young took the lead. We followed her to the entrance of the river walkway. I'd come here almost every single day, but this was my first time accompanied by someone, much less several strangers with whom I was about to go see long-legged river fowl. I cast around looking at the surroundings, as if everything was new. Ha-young, who was still in the front, walked with a purpose as if she knew exactly where to go. The two other women followed her silently. *Are grey herons easy to find though?* I wondered. *What if we don't see anything?* About ten minutes in, I began to worry this was a lost cause. Just then, Ha-young came to a standstill.

"This looks to be a good place," she said, pointing to a narrow wooden deck that lay across the river. As if by magic, one grey heron was loitering nearby, glaring at the surface of the water. I may have been in the rear but I had also been diligently observing the stream for any sign of the birds. *She's good*, I thought. *Does she have a bird sensor on her or something?* The other two women appeared nonplussed, almost as if this were a recurring thing. The older woman took a seat on a large flat rock by the edge of the walkway, while the college student leaned against the railing and turned on her camera. It clearly wasn't a high-end camera but the woman moved carefully, bringing it to her right eye, a grimace in her mouth.

"Make yourself comfortable, Yang-mi," Ha-young offered. She herself was standing on the deck, leaning on one foot. I squatted down awkwardly. This grey heron was much smaller than the bird Ha-young and I'd seen last time. I was no bird expert, but I suspected this one must be a young adult. Would it even know how to hunt?

The grey heron was standing against the tide, glaring at a spot near its feet. It stood there for a long time. In fact, it looked to be resting its head instead of actively hunting. But upon closer inspection, I saw I was wrong. The bird may have looked casual enough but there was an immense amount of focused concentration in its small, taut body, particularly in its piercing eyes and its sharp beak. It was concealing its lethal bloodthirst underneath its careless stance and was waiting patiently for the right moment to strike a single, clean, successful stroke. I marveled at its determination and stared at the bird, not daring to breathe. I couldn't afford to look away for even an instant.

"Oh!"

It was over in a flash. The grey heron leaned in and darted quickly into the water, and at the same time, I heard the whir of the camera shutter. In the instant it took the bird to slip in and out of the water, it had fetched something in its beak. I'd never realized there were such fat, large minnows in the river. The fish fought desperately, but it slithered down the throat of the bird in one fell swoop.

"Amazing," the older woman whispered softly. When I looked behind her, I saw her smiling and looking at me. She looked as proud as if she had been the one doing the hunting, not the bird. I probably had the same look on my face. The scene was mundane enough, just a bird catching a prey in its beak, but for some reason, the experience was incredibly moving—yes, *moving*. It wasn't just me who felt it. The four of us had all felt that shiver of excitement at the same time. This made me realize that our reaction was quite normal and to be expected, at least around these parts. I relaxed into the feeling.

"It looked quite young, but it's still a good hunter," I murmured in a low voice.

"Young, old, these herons are all excellent hunters."

"I think the younger ones are actually better at hunting. Just you watch, that one's going to catch some more."

Ha-young and the older woman murmured back in response. The younger woman, who had been peering into the camera's viewfinder, lifted the camera back up to her right eye. The left part of her face looked serious and determined.

We sat there watching the birds for a few more hours. They weren't always successful. One out of every five attempts was a failure but even then, the herons remained expressionless and stoic. After each attempt, whether successful or not, they went straight into concentrating for the next hunt. When the birds succeeded, we each let out a soft gasp of pleasure, and when they didn't, we groaned in frustration. Some passersby, curious to see what these four grown women were reacting to, stood behind us to watch for a while. Some kids came scampering into the water and splashed around, causing the bird to fly away. When it did, we slowly followed in pursuit. If it was too far away, we walked downstream and looked for another heron. Each time we did, I secretly worried we might not be able to find a bird this time, but Ha-young seemed to be gifted with some innate skill of locating grey herons. When she led our group to where the next grey heron was and pointed at it, we would fan out and take a comfortable position from where we could watch the bird.

Soon, the skies began to darken. The young college student waved her camera at Ha-young. It must have run out of battery.

"Let's call it a day. Since we have a new member, why don't we go for a short walk before saying goodbye?" Ha-young suggested. We got up from our seats, making sure to dust off our pants bottoms. We also remembered to gently pat the flattened patches of grass where we'd sat to revive the blades. Then we slowly headed upstream, back to where we came.

While slowly making our way to the bus stop in front of the old Sillim Theater, I learned that the older woman's name was Shim Dong-mi and the college student was Kang Hee-jin. I also learned that all three lived near the hill overlooking the intersection of Mirim Girls' High School, which was where I also lived. They had been meeting every other Sunday to watch herons for over six months now.

But the most surprising news broke when I told them my name.

"I'm Yang Yang-mi. I also live in Daehak-dong," I introduced myself briefly. At that, Hee-jin stopped in her tracks and peered at me.

"Wait, didn't you own a *banchan* shop? Yang-mi's Banchan?"

"Yes! Although I had to close the business," I replied, somewhat shocked to be recognized.

"I know that place, too!" Dong-mi chimed in. "It's near my house."

"I've shopped for food there myself!" Ha-young remarked. "You used to own that deli?"

I stared at the three women, not being able to say anything. It wasn't unusual to know the ins and outs in such a small neighborhood, including which business or shop had closed or opened nearby, but I was still taken aback that someone else remembered the name of my *banchan* shop, much less three people. Surprised and grateful, I kept opening my mouth to say something then closing it shut again. Dong-mi, however, landed the ultimate blow.

"I really liked your *banchan*. My husband enjoyed them, too."

It was a good thing I remembered to purse my lips firmly, as tightly as I could. That was the only thing that kept me from bursting into wailing sobs in front of three complete strangers. Realizing I had to say something in reply, I tried to force out a response but the insides of my throat felt swollen and hot. Instead, I stared awkwardly at Dong-mi, willing myself not to cry, but with tears brimming in my eyes.

"Hey, hey, hey! What's going on?" Dong-mi, understandably confused, came a step closer towards me but I couldn't do anything except struggle to fight back the tears. So I stood there like an ugly statue in the middle of the street, clenching my jaw tight and lowering my chin, all the while furiously commanding myself to stop it, for the love of God, stop embarrassing yourself in public, think of something funny instead! Perhaps I hadn't experienced anything fun in so long. I couldn't think of anything, and, despite my desperate attempts, the tears finally came.

Hee-jin, who had been standing there just as awkwardly as the rest of us, suddenly dashed off. I looked up to see where she was heading. She was running towards the Lotteria burger joint next to the subway exit. Roughly, she pushed the doors and ran inside, then, before the door had a chance to close, ran back out. I could see a wad of napkins clutched in her fist as she came running back towards us from the crowd.

Breathing hard, Hee-jin offered me the napkins. I fumbled with the napkins and folded them once before dabbing them at my eyes. They smelled of hamburgers. I knew I should thank Hee-jin but the salty, nutty smell of burgers pushed me over the edge, and in the end, I burst into sobs before the three women.

"Things don't work out sometimes. Life is funny like that," Dong-mi sighed, after I'd tearfully told them the entire story of what happened to my failed business.

It was completely dark by then, the sun having set a long time ago, but the air still felt warm against our cheeks from the hot afternoon sun. Small winged insects shot up like fireworks into the pools of light cast by the streetlamps. We were sitting at a small park close to the Mirim Girls' High School intersection. We hadn't decided to come here, our feet simply brought us to a place that was close to where the four of us lived that was also an ideal place to carry on a conversation. Passersby glanced at the four of us sitting in a row on a single park bench. I didn't blame them. It was unusual to see a grown woman blubbering late at night surrounded by three other grown women listening intently.

Shim Dong-mi got up from her seat and headed over to the swing set. I assumed she was going to ride one but instead, she walked around stroking the steel frame and poles. She was caressing the swings lovingly as if they were valuable to her. After a long beat, she spoke.

"I felt that way when I was raising my kids. Some things you can't ever have your way, no matter how hard you try."

"Yes, yes. Everyone has those experiences. I had one, too," Ha-young joined in. I sat silently, my head bowed. Earlier, I couldn't stop myself from spilling out the story of my business almost as if I were hurling something up from inside of me, but once it was over, I was feeling distinctly embarrassed for having bared my soul so shamelessly. I also remembered having bawled like a baby in the middle of the street. Dong-mi, with her back to us, continued.

"That's when I started bird-watching. And I think it really helped."

Bird-watching? I looked up quizzically at this sudden change of topic. Dong-mi was still stroking the steel frame of the swings.

"My youngest is in junior high now. He is an incredibly difficult boy, so much for me to handle. Watching those birds, I couldn't help but wonder how they must have been taught so well by their parents to be such excellent hunters. I was envious of their secret but later, I finally realized. Some things can be taught but some things must be learned by oneself, on their own."

"Yes, I've learned quite a few things too, from watching those herons," Ha-young said, standing up. Taking long strides with her thin, scrawny legs, she headed over to where Dong-mi was. She looked as if she was gearing up to give a speech.

"I regretted marrying young. I had several opportunities to break up with him, but I missed those windows and ended up getting married. But when you see those herons, you notice how they always seem to get the timing just right. When they feel they've caught enough fish in one part of the river, they know when to give up and fly to another spot. When they feel a spot isn't working out for them, they fold and fly elsewhere. I wondered how they were always so savvy like that. But now I think I know. After several failed attempts, they know they have to give up. When they realize that, they make a clean break and fly away. They fly away. Just like that. I feel they're wiser than humans in that sense."

With that, Ha-young gave a small cough and continued, "I've always wanted to say that out loud one of these days. Yang-mi's story gave me that chance."

I knew that was my cue to say something. But again, I couldn't bring myself to speak.

I had a story about the herons, too, a lesson learned from watching the birds. The grey herons were handsome fowl, long and sleek and skilled in hunting their prey. But what was most memorable to me was their reaction to a failed hunt, the way they would react when they come up empty after a long time concentrating on the river and finally making that strategic dive. If it were me, or anyone else for that matter, I'd have glanced around embarrassedly, coughing a few times, to see if anyone had seen my mistake. But the herons never did. It wasn't that they dismissed the idea of failure, it seemed more as if they gave equal weight to both success and failure. The birds didn't seem overjoyed when they succeeded. To them, all that mattered was to choose a strategic spot, concentrate, then swoop in for the kill. Whatever happened after that had equal bearing. It was that stoic quality of the birds that impressed me, that filled me with envy. I wasn't sure if humans were even capable of such nonchalant stoicism but I hoped to at least become more like them, perhaps one day achieving that quality in myself. But I didn't know how to express this feeling to the other women, to describe it in a way that did this feeling justice. In fact, I worried that any attempt to voice my feelings would lead to a horrendously embarrassing experience for all of us involved. Like a goldfish pulled out of water, I sat there opening and closing my mouth a few times, then managed a weak, "Yeah, I can see that."

Just then, Hee-jin stood up slowly, after remaining quiet all this time and listening to our conversation while stroking her camera. Maybe she had something she wanted to say, I thought, but Hee-jin walked past me and the other women to where the slide was. Suddenly, she began climbing the slide from the bottom up. When she arrived at the top, she squatted down and grabbed her camera. She cocked her head to one side, as if asking us for permission, then, before we had a chance to say anything, began clicking away.

"Hey, you should've warned us!"

Dong-mi and Ha-young came running back to where I sat. They brought their faces close to mine, with one of them draping her arm across my shoulders. Almost by instinct, I raised both hands in the shape of the letter "V" and looked up to where Hee-jin was. I realized how ridiculous I must have seemed, after recounting the sad story of a failed business and crying before a bunch of strangers and now smiling up at the camera. But this feeling wasn't all bad. I sat there, grinning.

We said our goodbyes after agreeing to meet back at the bus stop near Sillim Theater two Sundays later.

I was to take a right from the park, while the three women had to take a left. We nodded to one another and were about to go our separate ways when suddenly a thought came to me like a stroke of lightning. Even before I had the chance to mull over the thought to consider whether it was a good idea, I was already running madly toward the other women who were already halfway up the street.

"Wait! Wait a minute!"

I must have run maybe a dozen steps or so, but given that I had been sobbing for some time, I became completely out of breath. I looked at the three confused women, trying to catch my breath.

"Would you like to take some *banchan* ingredients home with you? Stuff like dried cuttlefish, some anchovies, maybe some dried shrimp and seaweed for broth?"

The women remained silent, looking down at me. Embarrassed, I continued headlong, "I have a ton of leftover ingredients at home, so..."

As if on cue, the three women burst out laughing.

"*That's* why you came running up here?"

"I thought there was an emergency!"

"I wouldn't say no to free food! I have a big family to feed, so anything you can save for me, I'll take."

I wasn't sure why they found this to be so uproariously funny, but I waited until they had their chance to laugh it out. I admit I chuckled a few times as well. I became happy at the thought that the three women would soon be back on this street again in a few minutes, each bearing an armful of food.

After our laughter had died down, we turned and headed in the direction of my apartment. The streetlamps were casting a warm orange glow over the street. From an open window in the distance, we could hear the sound of someone doing the evening dishes. I led the way, my shoes making a *tap-tapping* sound on the pavement. When I turned around, I saw three strange yet affectionate faces behind me. Without having to look, I knew they would be right there.

MOON CHEESE AND BISCOTTI

It was five minutes past the hour by the time a man in a dark-blue jacket walked in. He went around the room distributing slips of paper and a pen to each of us. They're always late, these therapist and doctor types. They must be taught to disregard patients' time when they're in medical school. I glared at the man's hairy hand as he thrust a piece of paper at me. Then, realizing how strange I must have seemed, I quickly looked away. I was completely sound of mind and didn't want to appear like I belonged here as one of the patients. As I told myself to act normal however, I became confused as to what normal would even look like in this context.

After the man finished handing out the slips of paper, he returned to the front of the room.

"Hello, everybody!" he greeted us.

Half the people in the room were paying more attention to the pens and paper than to him.

"My name is Meatball Spaghetti, and I'll be guiding you throughout today's writing therapy session," the man continued. "You can call me Meatball for short. Pleased to meet you all." With that, he gave a deep, exaggerated bow. Like he was a comedian who believed he had just completed the funniest bit. Of course, no one laughed. This made me sad, and with this sadness evident in my face, I turned to look at the woman next to me. She was spitting out something from her mouth. Something fell on the piece of paper she was holding. It was a bit of fingernail.

The man continued as if nothing had happened, as if he were used to this sort of non-reaction.

"No need to be frightened. Just think of this experience as a chance to make friends. You'll be teaming up in pairs and engaging one another in conversation. That's all. I'm not going to draw your blood or stick electrode pads on your arms."

He grinned foolishly. For the second time today, I felt sad. But instead of looking around the room trying to find someone to share in my emotion, I opted to sit still and stare blankly at Meatball.

"Why don't we begin by coming up with nicknames for ourselves? It could be anything, could be your favorite food, favorite person, whatever. For our sessions, we'll be calling each other by the nickname of your choice. I'll give you five minutes to think of a name."

Twirling my pen over the piece of paper, I wondered whether I'd made the wrong choice selecting writing therapy over swimming or even choir therapy. But my gut was way too big to be revealed in a swimming pool, even accounting for the fact I was in my mid-thirties, and the thought of having to sing before an audience was horrifying. That had left me with only one option. And now I had to come up with a nickname and write it down on this blank scrap of paper. Fortunately, I was immune to situations that demanded I write on the fly, given how I had to face them often as part of my job. I had a few tricks up my sleeve on what to do when I was at a loss for what to write. I chose the strategy of "procrastinating until the very last possible moment." There were now four minutes left.

There were roughly ten people in the room, seated in a circle. Only one of them looked to be legitimately crazy. She was a woman, and had ripped the piece of paper to shreds the instant the therapist handed one to her, then made a little pile of paper strips as if she were building a campfire. The therapist pretended to walk by the room again and surreptitiously handed her another piece of paper. I was familiar with how these therapy sessions usually went, and I prayed that I wouldn't have to partner with that psycho.

A while later—definitely much longer than four minutes later—the therapist collected our slips of paper.

"When I call your name, please stand up and briefly introduce yourself. It doesn't have to be long. Or if you'd rather not introduce yourself, you don't have to."

Self-introductions. I felt anxiety settling in the pit of my stomach. Self-introductions are hard even for sane folks. It would be easier to ask people to break out in dance or take off their clothes, because at least that way the person *making* the request could be made to look like the crazy one. Even so, the art of introducing yourself to strangers is a necessary practice in our society. Although that's precisely the reason self-introductions are so hard.

"Yogurt Jelly?" the therapist called out. A youngish woman sitting in one corner gingerly stood up.

"HiIloveyogurtjellyandalsoblueberryjellyandCokeflavoredjellytoo.YesterdayIhadblackpepperflavoredjelly." She said the words really fast, all in a blur. It sounded like she was chirping like a bird instead of voicing actual words. But the therapist smiled kindly at her.

"Good work. That was great. I love jelly, too. If you ever

find yourself in Sweden, I must insist you try some of their Swedish jelly. It's awesome. Next, Canned Beans?"

As he called out our names, the others stood up one by one to give their weird crazy talks while I sat there worrying over what to say. How should I best communicate to these psychos that I was completely sane and normal without any hint of mental illness whatsoever? I came up with several options but each one made me sound crazier than the last. When I was finally called ("Magic Cactus?") I stood up and said, "I write monthly horoscopes for a fashion magazine under the pseudonym Magic Cactus. If you'd like a subscription, let me know. I can get you a thirty percent discount if you sign up for a year's subscription. I like to travel and recently went to Nha Trang with my mother. That's in Vietnam. It was great. I live in the neighborhood, so I hope we can get to hang out. If you feel like grabbing a beer sometimes or you're bored and would like to go for a walk, let me know."

I thought I must have sounded like an unstable idiot and quickly sat down. In fact, almost everything I said was a lie. I don't have the authority to offer discounts on the magazine. I hate to travel. I don't even live nearby. And I certainly didn't want to hang out, much less have a conversation, with any of the people here. If one of them were to suggest going for a beer, I might bite his ear off.

"Horoscopes! That's such an interesting profession. Would you say you're an astrologist then? I'm a Gemini. What does my horoscope look like this month?" the therapist asked.

All Geminis will die a most gruesome death before the day has passed, I wanted to say out loud but didn't. I was still sane enough to know that my role here was to smile shyly and have him move on. I pretended to listen closely to what the others had to say, but in reality I was hoping that every person here would be struck by a sudden bout of memory loss. I knew I would spend the rest of the day regretting the stupid speech I gave. But then I thought even Barack Obama and Martin Luther King Jr. and other great orators would typically feel a slight sense of unease and embarrassment after introducing themselves. That made me think that, somehow, the embarrassment I was feeling right now was also completely normal and natural.

I may be sitting among these weirdos but I'm completely sane and did not have any mental disorders (other than the mild levels of paranoia that everyone living in today's society must endure). The only thing that was special about me was that I could talk to rocks. That's the only reason I was sitting here today. Do you believe that? I have a skill that the vast majority of humanity does not possess, yet instead of being praised and admired for this superpower, I'm treated like a lunatic.

When I announced that I was going to join this treatment program, my mother wept, overjoyed. The decision was my present for her sixtieth birthday. I realize it sounds bizarre to say I'm checking in to a psychiatric clinic as a birthday present for my mother. But except for one unhappy stint over ten years ago, I have never once turned to modern medicine for any kind of support, and my mother often spoke of how heartbroken she was because of me. The fact that I couldn't find anyone to marry, how I couldn't hold down a decent job, and even my obesity was all chalked up to my mental illness.

I knew she was wrong. I was merely a confirmed bachelor and magazine contributor who happened to like hamburgers and pizza.

My mother refused to give up. Several times, I came home to find her having tea with a stranger in our house, clutching a silk handkerchief in her hand which she used to dab at her wet eyes. As I removed my shoes in the foyer, her trembling words would float out to me.

"This is a psychotherapist who has come to help you. Talk to her."

With that, she would bring a tray piled with enough cookies and fruit to feed a group of ten, then retreat quietly to her bedroom where she would proceed to softly—but very clearly—sob. I was the one who wanted to break down and cry. But instead of a handkerchief, I would reach for the cookies and proceed to remove their individual wrappers. *Crunch crunch.*

After so many of these encounters, I came to have a good understanding of the business model of these so-called psychotherapists.

"Your mother told me a little about you," they would begin. "So, you can hear rocks talking to you?"

Most therapists spoke very little and tended to speak in circles even when they did. They were clearly trying to have me do most of the talking. *When did you first start hearing the rocks speak? Why do you think you can hear them? How does that make you feel?*

For the sake of my poor mother, who would be on the other side with her ear to the door, I answered their inane questions as diligently as I could. They would scribble in their notebooks and wear a strange expression somewhere between a frown and an awkward smile. I realized later that the expression meant they were attempting to analyze my symptoms.

Their next question was always the same, down to the last word.

"Why do you think only you can hear the rocks?"

The question is borderline offensive, something akin to: *So, you think you've got some kind of superpower or something?* I try to be as polite as I can.

"I can't help that I'm able to hear them."

At that, all the therapists would invariably reach into their pockets and hand me a small pebble. It's as if they planned this.

"Can this stone talk to you then? Can you tell me what it's saying?"

Of course, not all rocks can talk. If they did, I'd go insane from all the noise I'd have to filter through. It was similar to how not all humans could ride unicycles or do headstands. When asked how some rocks are able to talk to humans, I gave the same answer I always did. ("I'm not sure. I've found I can communicate with some of them, but not all of them.") But the pebbles the therapists thrust at me were all non-verbal, a fact which I had to inform them of.

"This rock must not know how to talk to humans."

When I said that, the therapists would place the pebbles back in their pockets, with a look that said they expected as much. Feeling vaguely guilty, as if I'd come up with a lie or an excuse, I would reach for another cookie. I didn't know if the pebbles genuinely couldn't speak or if they could but didn't want to at the moment. We don't go up to a quiet person and randomly ask them if they're mute or deaf. If someone did such a thing, that person should be the one in a psychiatric ward.

Soon, I became skilled at dealing with these therapists and even began entertaining myself by messing with them. For example, I would purposely wait until almost the end of the session to finally mention my father, not unlike saving the best dessert for last.

"Frankly, I don't know what my dad looks like," I would begin. "He passed away when my mother was still pregnant with me. There isn't a single photograph of him. I heard that I look a lot like him though. Maybe they had McDonald's and Pizza Hut in those days, too."

At that, the Freudian therapists would finally look up, their eyes gleaming. Ah, the expression of pure joy and relief that would sweep over their faces at the mention of my father! I actually felt proud for them on their behalf. *Really? Can you tell me more about your father? Do you miss your father? Do you often have thoughts of your father? Do you feel a duty to protect your mother as her only child?*

To be sure, my mother is one of those types of people who certainly does not require any outside protection. She's sixty years old and yet continues to helm a famous fashion magazine as its editor-in-chief and is more knowledgeable than I am on post-2000 trends. Her life, simply put, revolves around her Apple watch, aerial yoga, vegan food, and front row seats to Chanel's private fashion show. The combined followers across her different social media channels including Twitter, Facebook, Instagram, and YouTube vastly outnumber the population of the city of Seoul. Last month, she was named one of the 100 most influential Korean female entrepreneurs and received a crystal trophy for the honor. Everyone admires and respects her. And she has retained all of her youthful beauty. I am aware how it must sound to have a 30-something bachelor son describe his mother as beautiful, but she is, objectively speaking, quite beautiful. The fact that she does not have a husband was never an obstacle in her life or career. In fact, the only shortcoming she does have is that she has a single, obese, middle-aged son who can talk to rocks.

Once the therapists get wind of my mother's fame, they quickly change tack. *Isn't it difficult living in the shadow of such an amazing woman? Have you ever wanted to escape her influence?* And et cetera. They then launch into long diatribes about the Oedipus complex or gender roles. To me, these concepts were not unlike the old condoms I'd kept in my wallet for the past twenty years. I'm aware they exist but have no idea why they exist and I'd likely never have any use for them.

Dozens of therapists came and went, with Mother dutifully having baked at least a hundred plates of brownies for them, and yet I could still talk to rocks. By then, I learned not to tell anyone of my special ability, and every time I wanted to speak to a rock, I made sure there was no one around to hear me. But whenever my mother asked, I always chose to be truthful.

"Do you still have those rock friends of yours?"

"Sadly yes, I'm still best friends with them."

She would have caught on if I'd lied anyway, and besides, I didn't want to lie to her. I don't know why. Maybe those therapists would point to this as evidence that I did indeed suffer from an Oedipus complex.

The one and only time I visited an actual psychiatric clinic, I was diagnosed with having delusional disorder. Later, at home, I looked up the definition for delusional disorder in the *Diagnostic and Statistical Manual of Mental Disorders* as compiled by the American Psychiatric Association. The first line of the definition read that the disorder had the feature of having one or more "non-bizarre" delusions. I took it as good news that the doctor who diagnosed me considered me non-bizarre. If my delusions were categorized as bizarre, I'd have been diagnosed as being schizophrenic. Good. At least I wasn't bizarre. And honestly, didn't everyone have some sort of non-bizarre disorder anyway? I thought it much better to talk to rocks than, say, ferociously chewing everything that's popped into one's mouth or not being able to sit still without shaking their leg. Much better.

I was seventeen when I learned I could speak to rocks. At seventeen years old, I was pretty much human garbage. My weight in kilograms was almost as much as my height; I sported an unsightly buzz crew cut and my skin was pimply and nasty. I couldn't tell you the rules of any sports game to save my life, and my grades were below average. The only thing I had going for me was my unfounded belief that this phase in my life would end soon. Anyone who's been regularly bullied in school would know. The true humiliation lies not in the fact you were beaten up, but in letting it show that it had an impact on you. I was a master at ignoring the guys who made my life hell (or so I believed). When they chucked my shoe into the toilet, I thought it must have been done by a poltergeist. When no one refused to team up with me for an assignment, I believed I must have superhero-like abilities to push people away. Of course, these defense mechanisms didn't work. The universe attacked me with the full force of all the unhappiness it could unleash, and, given my huge size, I was an easy target. When I woke up in the morning, I wished the day would end quickly and went to bed praying that the world would end tomorrow.

Then, one summer, I was hiding in the parking lot behind the school, away from some kid who wanted to fondle my overly large breasts (like most obese men, I suffered from gynecomastia, or enlarged male breasts). It seemed at that moment no one could save me from that boy. All I could do was pray that he would lose interest in me, turn around, and go home to jerk off in the privacy of his home. But I knew from experience that these prayers always went unanswered. It didn't take him long to find me.

"Here you are, Heifer!" The boy cried gleefully.

I pretended to pick something off the ground and peer at it with interest, as if I weren't hiding from him. That was my last attempt at saving some measure of my dignity. But it only made me look more like a loser. I knew the kid was going to start raining punches on my head and stomach. Just then, I heard a voice from inside my fist.

"Throw me! Throw me at him!"

I didn't have time to think. Like an enchanted scarecrow, I threw the stone that was in my hand, making direct contact with the kid's forehead.

I don't care if you don't believe me.

The stone was sharp and jagged. The bully had to get four stitches, and I had to explain to my teacher and mother that

I hadn't intended on hitting the guy on the head. Of course, I didn't inform them that it was the stone that ordered me to throw it. My mother was thrilled that I'd finally manned up. She advised me to do the same thing next time those bullies came at me again.

When the jerk returned to school, bandaged up, I was predictably beaten to a pulp. In fact, after the incident, my school life became infinitely worse. But I was able to withstand those difficulties because of my newfound hobby. I began going around picking up every stone and rock I could find to talk to it. *Hello? Can you hear me? Answer me. I can understand you. Please.*

It was like a message broadcast by the last man on a post-apocalyptic Earth to the rest of humanity. Fortunately, some of the rocks did speak back to me. Not all of them did, but I was able to find many new friends. I tried to engage them in conversation, then, if I didn't feel like we had good chemistry, threw the rock far away. That's how I chose my friends. My pockets became full of them. I believed I'd been given a superpower only bestowed on the most severely bullied kids of the world.

Ironically, it was only after I began making these new friends that I realized how lonely I had been. I had no idea I'd been lonely all those years. It was simply my default state. Now that I had friends, every day was filled with wonder. I couldn't believe I had someone to talk to now: "There's a new PlayStation out." "I like Green Lantern more than Wolverine." How had I fared all those years without anyone to talk to?

My oldest friend was a trachyte rock I met when I was twenty-three years old. It's a handsome piece of rock in a deep chocolate color flecked with white mineral particles. I called it Scott, because it reminded me of the biscotti my mother would bake sometimes. Scott was an excellent and wise friend.

It was Scott who told me it would be smarter of me not to reveal to people that I could speak to rocks. His logic was that it was always wiser not to reveal any extraordinary abilities to others. He was right. Spiderman and Batman chose to assume other identities during the day and hide their true selves. When people are faced with something that's different, or new, or incomprehensible, they either ignore it or despise it, rather than work on acceptance. I wasn't interested in being understood or sympathized with by others. My world was already complete. The only things I needed in life were Scott and a delivery of one large-sized supreme pizza and a bottle of Coke every three days or so.

After our last group therapy session, someone must have complained the room was too hot. The next time we met, the room was much cooler. Last time, the desks and chairs were arranged in a circle. This time, they were placed two and two together (hospitals always know the easiest and best way to coerce their patients into such pre-determined seating arrangements). The man sitting next to me was a strapping, tall fellow who appeared to be the most normal person in the room. We had just introduced ourselves to one another. He said his name was Cooker.

"Cooker? You must like to cook," I said, to which the man threw back his head and laughed uproariously. I withdrew into myself (exaggerated displays of emotion were typical signs of a mental disorder).

"No, Cooker is the name of a robot. Have you heard of *Wallace and Gromit*?"

"You mean the clay animation?" I asked. "I think I watched it when I was little."

I didn't know much about *Wallace and Gromit* other than the fact there was a stupid-looking dog in the show. But when I told the man I'd seen the show, he became excited and started jumping around like a crazy person.

"Yes, that's it! It's a clay animation series made in England. Wallace is the human, and Gromit is the dog. There's also another character, Cooker! He's a robot. Do your remember Cooker?"

"I'm sorry but I don't recall that much of the show."

Of course, I wasn't sorry in the least. I was concentrating hard on ways to have the two-hour therapy session go by as quickly as possible. I couldn't believe I had to spend one-twelfth of my day in this meaningless exercise. I wanted to go home. I had a ton of stuff to do. I'd only made up the Taurus predictions for next week and had eleven more to go. I had to take our clothes out of the dryer before Mother came home. After that, I had to unwind with Scott and tell him about my day. I was planning on going on a trip tomorrow, so I also had to do some packing. A few months ago, I'd passed a riverbank that looked to be full of hematite rocks and had reminded myself to go back for a visit soon. Rocks rich in iron tended to be sensitive and thoughtful, making them excellent friends for Scott as well. Just then, the man next to me grabbed my hand. I had to stop myself from hurling a punch at him.

"I'm so glad we met! I'd never met anyone who likes *Wallace and Gromit*. I had a good feeling about you when you introduced yourself to the group last week, and now we're friends! I hope we can be good friends. I live near here, too!"

I'd only told him I was aware of *Wallace and Gromit*, not that I liked the show. I was about to point this out to him as I attempted to wriggle free of his grasp, when the therapist appeared behind me (therapists are skilled at moving cat-like without a sound).

"Wow! Look at you two, making friends already? Great! That's a great start. It's only a little awkward in the beginning, am I right?"

Cooker grinned broadly as if he'd just received the compliment of a lifetime, and the therapist beamed at him as well. The scene would have made an ideal advert for a mental health clinic. Goosebumps broke out on my skin. For the next two hours, I had to sit there, my mouth clamped shut, as this man went on and on about *Wallace and Gromit*. I learned that the show had a total of five episodes, and that the robot Cooker appears in the first episode, "A Grand Day Out." I also learned the man had watched that episode no less than over a thousand times. He told me how Wallace, the eccentric inventor, built a spaceship to fly to the moon and taste its cheese, and about the robot Cooker, who dwelled on the cheese moon and was its protector.

"Yes. I remember. It was quite interesting." That was all I said, but the man didn't seem to pick up on my clearly disinterested tone. Instead, he barreled on with his story. I was also made uncomfortable by the therapist, who snaked around the room eavesdropping on all the conversations, sometimes joining in. My mood was souring more and more by the minute.

As the session wound down and the man asked me for my number, the day reached fresh new lows.

"I had so much fun today. Can I text you? I know a great pub where we can go for beer," said the man cheerily, as he tucked his phone, which contained my number, back into his bag. It was a good thing I'd worn my shirt with the front pocket. If Scott hadn't whispered, "Calm down. He's just a nutcase," from inside the pocket, I'd have beaten this idiot to within an inch of his life then set fire to the entire building. Scott, ever the wise friend.

But the tragedy was far from over. That night, as I was packing a baseball cap into my luggage, I heard my phone ring. I thought it was the magazine's offices. The only people I could think of who would call me at such a late hour were magazine editors. But I was wrong.

"Hello! It's me, Cooker! I hope I didn't wake you!"

The man screamed into the phone as if he were speaking from one end of the universe to the other. When I remembered who he was, my mood soured again.

"No, you didn't. Is something the matter?"

"Not at all! Are you busy? If not, what say we go for a beer?"

"Oh, I'm sorry but I'm very busy right now. Extremely busy. Extremely so. Barely have time to breathe."

"Really? What are you up to?"

I should have hung up the phone then and there. But just then, my mother walked in with a load of my freshly laundered boxers from the dryer. She was taken aback by the sight of me on the phone this late at night. Cooker's voice was booming from the phone, like a disaster message blaring from loudspeakers. My mother could hear every single word.

"Oh… I uh… I was packing for a trip," I mumbled. "I have so much to do. I'm a little swamped."

"A trip? Where to?" Cooker screeched. "That sounds great! The weather is perfect for a trip!"

"Oh... Um... I was thinking... I was thinking of going to a river. I know a place."

"That's great! A river! I've been wanting to go see a river. I love to go fishing. Are you traveling with anyone?"

I tried to avoid looking at my mother, but I thought I could distinctly hear the sound of her raising her eyebrows. She was so surprised she forgot to put down the load of boxers. *Is someone actually offering to accompany my son on a trip? My deranged, morbidly obese, confirmed-bachelor son?*

"Hello? Hello!"

Cooker, Mother, Cooker, Mother. Humans typically make the worst decisions in times of extreme stress and anxiety. That's how we're wired. We watch helplessly, sweating profusely, as we plunge headfirst into a terrible situation of our own making.

From inside my pocket, Scott murmured, "This is going to be interesting."

The weather couldn't be more fantastic, and the breeze was refreshingly cool against our skin. As I'd suspected, most of the rocks scattered near this river contained traces of iron. Jagged, copper-colored rocks were strewn across the riverbank. If I could, I'd have gladly booked into a hotel nearby to check out the place at more length.

"Wow, this place is great!" Cooker chirped. "Although, why are these rocks so red?"

If it weren't for the incessantly chattering Cooker who was following me around like a baby chick after its mama hen, this trip would have gone down as the best thing that happened to me this second half of the year, one that wouldn't have necessitated Google searches such as *how to kill someone without getting caught*.

"It's so cool that your hobby is studying the Earth's crust! Seriously, *so* amazing. I hope I'm not getting in your way. Why don't I go over there and find a good spot for fishing? With fishing, it's always important to find the best spot. Once you have the spot, all you have to do is sit and wait for a few hours. For the fish. Although sometimes, you end up finding other weird stuff."

Grinning stupidly, Cooker turned and wandered off to a place further away. Over one shoulder, he'd slung a black fishing-gear bag almost as big as he was and was carrying a fishing net with his other hand. As he gingerly picked out his way among the sharp rocks, I couldn't help but think how he reminded me of a lunatic tottering away, although he looked just as insane seen from the front.

When I was sure he was out of earshot, I turned my back to him and got straight to work. What I had to do wasn't too difficult. I only needed to pick up the rocks that caught my eye.

"Hi there. Can you hear me? If you can, please say something."

The first rock I picked up didn't respond. But I wasn't disappointed. The only things I needed for this task were a pair of strong knees that could withstand hours of crouching down and a good measure of patience. If humans gave up after their first failed attempt, we wouldn't have come this far collectively as a species. I gave the rock plenty of time to decide whether to respond to me or not, gazing at it considerately.

Then, once it became clear the rock was going to stay mum, I carefully placed it back where it belonged. Then I turned to the next candidate.

"Hey, can you hear me? I can talk to you."

"Hi, will you say something? This is my friend Scott."

"Isn't this weather something? I'm not from around here."

I was repeating the same words over and over again but I wasn't bored in the least. If only making small talk with humans over cocktail parties and dinner receptions were this interesting. When, after the fifteenth attempt, I finally stumbled upon a rock that talked back to me, I was so happy I almost shouted in glee. The rock was a handsome hematite, as well-formed as a specimen in a museum.

"Am I really talking to a human male?" He had a low, thick voice. I could sense a hint of wariness in it, but I also detected unmistakably an undercurrent of warmth running through his voice, the kind of warmth that thoughtful, gentle beings tend to have.

"Hey! Thank you so much for talking to me," I gushed. "You have no idea how pleased I am. We're from far away, from a big city. Nice to meet you. You're very handsome."

"I've been here a long time but I've never seen a talking human before," the rock muttered. "The things you live to see..."

"Not everyone can talk to rocks. Actually, I believe it's just me."

"Oh, I see. That's interesting, very interesting."

Actually, the conversation wasn't all that interesting. But I was extremely excited, and so was Scott. It had been some time since we'd found a new friend, and the weather was truly spectacular. Besides, there were plenty of other rocks here that I hadn't had a chance to meet.

"What's it like here?" I asked.

"Same old, same old. The sun is nice and warm most days, but when it rains, the river overflows sometimes."

"It's awful to be covered in muddy water," Scott added helpfully. He seemed to like this new guy, which was rare for Scott as he tended to be picky in choosing friends. Rocks are simple and forthright creatures; after a few minutes talking to them, it's easy to see the kind of personalities they have. We sat down comfortably and carried on talking to the new rock.

The river, the sunshine, a new friend and an old companion. By then, I'd completely forgotten about the idiot Cooker, for the first time that day.

Just then, I heard a dull thud somewhere. I don't recall whether the splash came first or the scream, but when I turned around, I caught a glimpse of a big splash in the river.

"What's going on?" Scott asked in a bewildered voice. I brought my hand up to my forehead to shield my gaze from the sun and squinted into the distance.

"Help! HELP!"

Even before I heard the shouts, I was running towards him. It was Cooker. Cooker was thrashing around in the middle of the river!

"Don't move! Stay still!" I shouted as I ran. Of course, Cooker didn't stay still. He didn't want to sink. I saw his frightened face bobbing up and down in the water as the current slowly took him downstream. Not having time to take off my shoes, I frantically waded into the river.

"Grab my hand!"

I reached out to him and Cooker thrust himself toward me. But his gigantic body, now soaked as a sponge, was much heavier than I'd anticipated. I felt my feet slip from underneath me and the water sweep me up. The rough waters had claimed their second victim.

"Noooooo!"

We thrashed around in the muddy water, our arms and legs entangled. I suddenly remembered how I regretted not having chosen swimming therapy instead of writing therapy. If I'd opted for the other class, this idiot wouldn't have come into my life. But as with most regrets, this one didn't help my case any.

It felt like we'd been splashing around in the water forever, but it had been less than five minutes. When I came to, I saw that we were crouched on the riverbank, heaving and retching the muddy river water from our mouths like two rubber hoses.

"I'm sorry…" Cooker said in a tiny voice, after he'd had a chance to catch his breath.

"Are you insane? Why did you go in there?"

As I shot him a dirty look (FYI, calling a psycho insane was more fun than I thought), Cooker whimpered quietly, looking like a soggy wet biscuit.

"I'm so sorry. My hook got caught somewhere in the water…"

I could have drowned in the river because of this stupid bastard! I felt goosebumps on my skin. Cooker took off his dripping wet shirt and I saw his pale upper body. I wanted to smack him on the back. If I were a fast runner, I'd have smacked him then run off. I took off my own shirt and was about to squeeze it dry when I realized something was not right.

Scott!

Scott was missing! My shirt front pocket was empty. It had felt strangely light, devoid of his weight. I couldn't remember when I'd lost him.

"Cooker, did you see Scott?"

"Huh?"

"My rock. The rock that was inside my pocket! Did you see him or not!"

Instead of replying, Cooker stared at me. Silence. Water dripped from his hair. He didn't say anything. But I thought I could read his mind. *Poor fool... I thought he was sane, but I guess he's one of those schizos, too.* I wanted to kill him. But I didn't know how. He was taller and stronger than me, and I wasn't carrying a weapon. Besides, my priority was to find Scott, not kill Cooker. I forced myself to stay calm.

"When I ran over to you, I lost something very important to me. Will you help me find it? It's a small rock the size of my palm, brown with flecks of white."

Slowly, Cooker nodded. But he didn't seem to be taking this seriously. I couldn't even tell if he'd understood me or not. I didn't care. I turned and began scanning the ground.

"Scott! Scott! If you can hear me, please say something! Please!"

But there was only silence.

"Scott! Please!"

I groped around wildly but there was no Scott to be found. Just then, a terrible thought struck me. What if I'd lost him in the river? I let out a pained, feral cry then collapsed among the rocks. I began to sob. Scott hated being cold and hated muddy water most of all. I couldn't believe I'd lost Scott to those murky depths all because I was trying to save some madman!

"Hey, are you okay?" Cooker drew near and placed a hand on my shoulder. Roughly, I shoved it aside. In that moment, I felt I could kill him. I wanted to kill him in the most painful and gruesome way imaginable.

"I'm sorry..." Cooker said softly, but I wasn't listening. I was thinking of ways to save Scott. There was one option. I could go to the car, grab my phone, and call a professional diver. The river wasn't too wide or deep. I'm sure the diver would be able to find Scott. They are trained professionals. They'd have no trouble locating a small piece of rock. I had to think. Scott must be near here somewhere. I couldn't lose track of this spot.

"Cooker, do you mind standing here and not moving? I'm going to the car for my phone. Don't move."

Cooker's shoulders were heaving. He appeared to be crying.

"I'm sorry... I'm sorry... This is all my fault. It's my fault."

"Listen, just, can you stay here or not?"

At that, Cooker began bawling. "The therapist told me about you. He said you can talk to rocks," he heaved between sobs. "You said you're looking for Scott... That's your friend, isn't it? You just lost your friend, didn't you? I'm so sorry. I believe you. I'm sorry. I'll do anything to get your friend back."

I don't know what froze me to the spot as I heard those words. Maybe it's because this was the first time someone said they believed me. Although in this case, the someone was a dripping wet psycho looking like a melting ice cream cone. Or maybe I was just scared Cooker was going to move from the spot.

"I'm so sorry," Cooker sobbed. "I understand. I understand everything."

Should I break his legs to ensure he wouldn't move? Or should I run to the car first? Even now, Scott could be rolling away from me, writhing in agony in the cold, muddy water.

Meanwhile, Cooker had sunk to the ground and was all-out bawling.

"I understand! I really do!"

I didn't know what he meant by that, but Scott was my priority. I ran to the car, all the while shouting at Cooker to stay put. I didn't have to though, because Cooker was so miserable he didn't seem to be able to move.

Half hidden in the warm tub of lemon-scented bubbles, Scott sighed, "Friend, that was a long day."

I merely nodded as I'd just then taken a huge bite of stuffed cheese crust pizza.

It really was a long day just as Scott said. It took five hundred years to wait for the diver to arrive, another five hundred years to explain to him what Scott looked like, then a further two thousand years to explain why it had to be that specific rock and not the other thousands of similar rocks strewn on the riverbank, as the diver was quick to point out. Then there were dozens of failed attempts ("Is this the one?" "No, that's not like him at all! I told you he has white flecks. White!") but in the end, the idiot diver managed to locate Scott in the water, just ten meters away from the banks. As those three thousand years passed by, I aged significantly from the worry and anxiety that were eating away at me. The only thing that could restore me to my formerly sprightly thirty-something self was to lock myself and Scott in my room and gorge on pizza.

"I really thought I'd lost you," I said.

"Don't say that," Scott laughed. "It was awful down there."

"Yes, I'm sure it was."

Cooker had paid the diver. (The diver left after stealing quizzical glances at us two full-grown men sobbing over a wet rock.) While I toweled Scott dry, Cooker hung around.

"Um... Would it be okay if I introduced myself to your friend?"

Overjoyed at having found Scott, I must have let go of one percent of my rage towards Cooker. I allowed him to touch Scott. Carefully, Cooker placed Scott on his palm and spoke.

"Hello, Scott. My name is Cooker."

Scott quipped back, "You look dreadful. Almost like you're stark raving mad."

I burst out laughing. Cooker looked up at me and asked, "What? What? What did he say?"

"Nothing. Scott says he's pleased to meet you too. He says he looks forward to getting to know you."

At that, Cooker grinned wide.

"Me, too! Scott, you're a great guy, er, rock!"

We got into the car and came home. On the way, we talked variously about women, philosophy, comic books, and other subjects. Cooker did most of the talking, and I translated

Scott's responses to him. Although I took care not to translate all of the sarcastic quips Scott made.

We were nearing the city limits when Cooker spoke, "Listen, I want to tell you something since I think we've grown somewhat close."

Wearing a grave expression, he continued, "Don't you want to know why I attend those therapy sessions?"

Honestly, I didn't. But Cooker didn't wait for me to respond.

"I was eight years old when I first watched *Wallace and Gromit*. That night, I had a dream. I dreamed I was flying to a moon made of cheese. It was such a vivid dream that I couldn't stop thinking about it. I wondered if it really was a dream. The next night, I threw open my bedroom window. There was a full moon that night and, without thinking, I climbed up on the windowsill and jumped. I should have fallen and splattered my brains across the cement sidewalk but instead, I floated up and up. I was shooting up towards the moon, leaving a long trail of multicolored dust behind me. I felt so relaxed and comfortable, almost as if I'd always known how to fly but only realized it just then."

"Wow, this dude is totally wacko," Scott said. I didn't tell Cooker that, but I was thinking the same thing. I avoided Cooker's gaze by pretending to jiggle the car's GPS.

"It didn't take me long to arrive at the moon. The moon looked just like the moon in *Wallace and Gromit*. It really was made of cheese, from its surface down to its core. Gouda, Emmental, Comté, Cheddar… Every kind of cheese you could think of. I stuffed myself with the cheese. By the time I landed back on Earth, the sun had risen."

"…I see."

"I discovered some other things, too. For example, I could only fly to the moon on nights when there was a full moon. I couldn't bring any of the moon cheese back with me. And anytime I told anyone about this ability, they treated me like I was crazy. Of course, I didn't tell anyone. But each night there was a full moon, I had to explain to my family where I'd gone off to. In the end, my father sent me to that psychiatric center."

Cooker sniffed. Not knowing what to say, I cleared my throat and produced a weird, cracking sound. I thought I could understand what Cooker was going through, but, at the same time, I wanted to yell at him to stop talking nonsense. I still don't know what I had wanted to say to him in that moment. But I do recall how pitiful Cooker looked as he waved goodbye after I dropped him off.

"Scott, what do you think about what Cooker just told us?" I asked.

Scott yawned. "Nothing. I think he's lost his marbles."

"Yeah."

I closed the empty pizza box and stashed it away underneath my bed. I opened the window to let out the pizza smell. Mother would be home soon. If she asked how my trip went, I'd tell her it was swell, that I'd made a new nutjob friend.

"He says he can fly to the moon!" I'd tell her. "Isn't that something? He's even crazier than I am!"

The cool night air poured in through the open window. It was quite dark, and the moon hung round and fat in the sky, framed by twinkling stars. I felt tired, probably because I was so full.

"Scott, look at how big and round the moon is. It's giving me a craving for waffles."

I was laughing at my own silly joke when suddenly, I saw a sight that almost made me throw up the entire large pizza. Far off in the distance, I could clearly make out a black shape soaring high up into the sky, like a rocket. It was unmistakable.

"Scott! Do you see that?"

I pulled Scott from the bathwater and ran to the window. But there was nothing more I needed to say. The soaring, comet-like rocket was very obviously Cooker. Cooker was flying. Flying high and straight. Straight to the moon. Dazed, I stood there, staring at the sight. Was I losing my marbles? Had I spent too much time with a raving madman? Had I become infected, too? How could this be?

"Scott, Scott, do you see that?"

I shouted at Scott, my eyes still glued to Cooker. But Scott didn't respond.

"Scott?"

Still there was no reply. Scott was growing colder and colder in my palm.

"Scott? Hey, Scott?"

Standing there by the window, I stared dumbfoundedly at Cooker, then at Scott, then at Cooker. Back and forth. Back and forth. Cooker flew farther and farther away, until he finally disappeared into the moon, leaving no trace of the dust in his wake.

A FLAT WORLD

I was just about done with my lunch when I noticed a spot on the bottom of the rice bowl. It was a deep-blue spot that looked almost bruise-like. I paused my spoon mid-air and bent down to study the spot. As I did so, I saw the spot squirming and attempting to hide underneath the rice. What should I do? I glanced up at my stepmother sitting opposite me, intent on her meal. Shrugging, I finished the rest of the rice. I didn't think the spot was going to kill me, and besides, the rice tasted the same as it always did—the same, tired fried rice I ate every night, with the same mixed ingredients. After I finished the rice, I peered down and saw the spot was gone. Had it run away? Carrying the bowl to the kitchen sink, I checked the rest of the table, but there was nothing there. I must have eaten it. I washed the bowl. Maybe I hadn't washed the plates thoroughly enough last time. Maybe I shouldn't have watered down the dish soap to make it last longer. This time, I made sure to pump enough soap into the sponge and be extra firm in scrubbing the bowls and plates before I retired to my bedroom.

Since it was a Sunday, I didn't have to go to school. I didn't have anything to do or any friends to meet. I lounged in bed and counted the wires strung across the utility poles outside the window. I watched a couple of cat videos on YouTube. As I lazed around my room, I suddenly remembered something I had to do. I'd left my school uniform blouse in a tub of water this morning. I'd have to wash it and hang it up to dry if I wanted to wear it to school tomorrow. I gripped the bed attempting to lift myself up. But the sensation of the bed against my arm and the feeling of my feet touching the floor were a little off. I felt soft, almost like I was made of plush or as if my body had been covered by a thin film of springy material. Confused, I stood there in the middle of the room, thinking. Just then I realized what had happened. I'd become translucent.

Was it because of the spot I ate?

I sat down on the edge of my bed and thought. Nothing else stood out in my mind. I certainly hadn't consciously done anything to turn myself semi-transparent. The only slightly peculiar thing I could think of was the spot I ate with my fried rice. Maybe it was some kind of magical spot that turned you ghost-like. Did this mean my stepmother had also turned translucent? To find out, I had to go to the living room, but now that I was no longer solid, it was difficult to exert as much force as I used to. It took forever to summon the strength to grab a hold of the door handle, but each time I tried to twist it open, my soft, marshmallowy hand lost its grip. In the end I had to use both hands to get the door to open. When I finally managed to open it a crack, I slipped a few fingers through the gap to spread it open. By that point, I was exhausted. I collapsed on the floor with no energy left to venture outside and just gazed out across the living room. I could see the back of my stepmom's head as she sat watching TV. As always, she was sitting in a hunched position, slightly askew on the floor. She didn't appear to have gone translucent. I called out to her.

"Hey."

But she didn't respond. Had she fallen asleep? When I crept closer, I saw she was still awake and staring at the television with her eyes glazed over. If she were awake, why wasn't she saying anything?

"Hey!" I called out, a little angrily this time.

But even as I was practically up in her face by this point, she didn't flinch in the slightest. Even I could tell something was off about my voice. It sounded like a distant echo from a faraway place, like inside a deep cave or the outer realms of the universe. Wait a minute.

Noticing that the bathroom door was slightly ajar, I laboriously made my way inside and looked up at the mirror. What should have been a short, scrawny middle-schooler with a generous helping of acne on her forehead was instead, a ghost. I had gone fully transparent. I grabbed the sink and stood there staring into the mirror. Everything about the bathroom was just as it was—from the mildewy shampoo and conditioner bottles, to the broken tiles, and the Little Mermaid anti-slip stickers some kid who used to live here had stuck to the floor. And yet, I was no longer there. I couldn't be seen or heard. I had disappeared into thin air.

Hmm, I thought.

I was a little taken aback, but I wasn't sad. I wasn't sad because I had never had much of a presence to begin with. The world didn't seem to care whether I was there or not, or how I felt, or what I was craving, or who I was hanging out with. In effect, I was more or less in the same situation as I was before. Actually, I was better off. Now that I was practically a ghost, I could do the one thing I'd always wanted to do. Grinning, I headed back out to the living room and sat down in front of my stepmother. Looking directly into her eyes, I said,

"I hate you, too."

I thought she wouldn't hear me but then her arm flinched. I almost leaped up in shock, but she reached out and grabbed the remote to change the channel. Embarrassed, I sat back down.

"I really hate you," I repeated, although by that point the magic was gone.

My stepmom sat immobile before the TV for the next few hours. Watching TV was just about the only thing she ever did at home, but still. Hours? In the same exact position?

In the meantime, I kept myself busy, testing out different things about my new, transparent self. It had only been a few hours since I'd turned transparent, but I didn't feel any hunger pangs or the urge to go to the bathroom. I tried bumping hard against the wall but felt no pain, just a slight squishy sensation. But I couldn't pass through walls or objects. And my strength levels had shrunk to those of a tiny ant. I attempted to lift a corner of my comforter but it felt as heavy as a sack of rice. I tried lifting various other items in descending order of lightness—a poster, a hair tie—but soon tired and gave up.

Then I found I had nothing left to do. So I wandered around the house. I couldn't open any doors for the life of me, so instead I squeezed into the gaps of rooms where the doors were already open, which was just my bedroom, the living room, and the bathroom. My blouse was still soaked in the tub of water in the bathroom. Seeing it reminded me of school. I no longer had to go to school tomorrow. The thought cheered me up. School was never that fun.

The sun was setting by that point. My stepmother flipped through a few more channels then turned off the TV.

"Go-mi!" she shouted in the direction of my room.

When there was no response, she shouted again.

"Go-mi!"

Finally, she heaved herself up from the floor. Fascinated, I watched as she walked over to my room. How would she react once she realized I was missing? Would she be surprised? Angry? She peeked into my darkened bedroom. Reaching in, she flipped on the light switch. Lights flooded the empty room.

"Tada! I'm not there!" I shouted excitedly. Of course, this fell on deaf ears.

But my stepmother merely stood there, staring into the empty bedroom, then turned the lights off with a blank expression on her face. She turned the lights off in the living room and closed the kitchen window. I couldn't believe what I was seeing. Calmly, she headed into her own bedroom then slammed the door shut. From inside, I heard the rustling of her climbing into bed.

I kicked her bedroom door. I kicked as hard as I could, although the effect was as insignificant as a slight breeze against the doorframe. I cursed at her. *You must be soooo happy now that I'm gone! Bet you love this!* Tears sprang to my eyes. The tears were gelatinous and gooey like translucent jelly that dripped down to the floor where they glowed. Surprised despite the anger I was feeling, I quickly bent low to examine the texture of the tears. Then, embarrassed at how stupid I must have looked, I stopped kicking the bedroom door.

My new condition was not conducive to sleep. I lay in bed and willed sleep to come but I remained fully awake. Since I couldn't watch TV or look at my phone or read any books, I remained lying there in bed, thinking. I tried to think only good, happy thoughts. I didn't have to go to school tomorrow. I didn't have to take my final exams. I no longer had to clean the house or do the dishes or the laundry. My stepmother had made me do all the chores, citing her own partial blindness as an excuse, but she would have to cook for herself and do her own laundry now. I didn't have to be anything anymore. The thought cheered me up.

There was a terrible story behind my stepmother's half-blindness. It happened when she was in elementary school. Her family had gone on a trip together and on the drive home been involved in a three-car pile-up. She was eating roasted potatoes on a stick in the backseat when the accident occurred. The force of the accident ended up driving the skewer deep into her left eye. She was rushed to the hospital where doctors removed the broken-off piece of skewer and the grey mush that remained of her left eye. She was the only survivor of the accident and had lost her mother, her father, and her younger brother that same day. The fact that she lost her one eye was, relatively speaking, not so remarkable.

Ever since I heard the story, I hadn't been able to eat potatoes. Every time I attempted to bite into one, I pictured a sharp skewer bursting a thin leathery pouch that I imagined to be one's eye and experienced the sensation of having the pouch burst open inside my mouth. It wasn't just potatoes. The sight of any sharp object, such as knitting needles or syringes, and sometimes even mechanical pencils when I was feeling particularly sick or down, would be enough to set me off and make me want to run away. I first heard about my stepmom's accident when I myself was in elementary school. Although many years have passed and I'm now in the eighth grade, I still can't bear the sight of sharp objects. I couldn't imagine why anyone would have thought it okay to tell that story to a little girl.

It was, of course, my father who told me the story.

Just as vivid as the story is my recollection of the day when I heard it. I had returned home from school to find my father sitting in the living room with a woman wearing a patch over her left eye. Having always been a shy child, I stood frozen by the front door. Without looking in my direction, my father commanded me to come closer. Reluctantly, I approached the pair. The woman looked me up and down with her one good eye. She was small and crafty-looking, much like her eye. She was the first person in my life that I came to immediately hate at first sight. "She's going to be living with us from now on," my father said, as if it was the most natural thing in the world. Not fully understanding his words, I remained there, staring into the woman's face. My father, taking that to warrant an explanation of her eye patch, launched into the story of the skewer and the roasted potatoes. In fact, I remember my father ending the story with hearty laughter, as if he were proud of a good joke he'd just made. How did my stepmother react? I don't recall whether she burst out laughing with him or scolded him for having told such an inappropriate story to a child. I don't think she was pleased. She'd never once looked pleased, not in all the times I'd known her.

She and my father stayed together for quite some time, although they never had a wedding or filed for a marriage license. Their relationship wasn't peaceful, however. Father drank often and became violent when he did. Privately, I'd always thought the world would be better off without him. My curse must have worked, as he died not long after from cirrhosis of the liver, leaving me alone with my stepmom. Now that I was translucent and therefore said to barely exist, it was just her in the house. I thought that was unfair. I wanted to be the last one standing. Free and independent, without worry or care.

What's going to happen to me now?

Tossing and turning in bed, I tried to imagine a translucent future. But no matter how hard I thought, I couldn't imagine anything extraordinary occurring to me. With a body that couldn't be seen or heard, there was nowhere and no one I could turn to, thereby making my life a truly boring, miserable one, not unlike the life I had before I turned translucent. I lay there, tossing back and forth, bringing an end to what was an uneventful first day of being semi-transparent.

My stepmom woke up late and struggled to fix herself a pot of instant ramen for breakfast. After washing her face, she headed out and returned late at night. I tried to leave the house through the gap in the front door that opened when she went out but failed miserably the first day, then for several days later, as I couldn't get the timing right. I was scared I would end up getting caught in the door and having to wait there for hours until she returned. Because my stepmom made sure to turn off the TV before she left, there was nothing for me to do in the house. As a result, I was bored out of my mind for the next few days.

Then Saturday came. After lunch, my stepmom sat watching TV. I sat a distance away, finally enjoying some television time, when suddenly the doorbell rang. My stepmom jerked, startled, which startled me. We didn't often have visitors. She leaned over and peered through the peephole.

"Who's there?"

"Hello, ma'am. I'm Go-mi's homeroom teacher, from school," a voice called out.

"Who?"

"I'm Go-mi's teacher."

I recognized the voice. It was my homeroom teacher. After a pause, my stepmother opened the door. My teacher was standing there. It felt strange to see her out in the wild like this. She had the distinct air of being a middle-aged door-to-door salesperson rather than a middle-school teacher. My stepmother must have thought the same since, instead of inviting her inside, she remained standing there, staring at my teacher.

"I'm sorry for bursting in on you like this," my teacher spoke. "But you wouldn't answer the phone. And Go-mi's phone is turned off."

My teacher was sweating. It must be hot outside. Still, my stepmother didn't ask her to come in. Rather, she stood steadfast, guarding the entrance and stared at my teacher. My teacher stared back at my stepmom's face, at the dirty disposable eye patch covering her left eye and the right eye rapidly darting to and fro to take in the scene.

"She's at her grandmother's."

My stepmother spoke, after a short, intense pause.

"She said she'd told the school already. Didn't you hear?" she added.

My teacher cocked her head to one side then parted her lips, as if to say something. She didn't look like she believed what she just heard.

"Go-mi? She's at her grandmother's?"

"That's right."

"Is something the matter? She shouldn't have these unexcused absences," my teacher said.

"There was… There was a funeral she had to attend."

"A funeral? Why aren't you with her?"

"I'm not her real mother."

It was my teacher's turn to shut up. My stepmom looked haughtily at her. *What a childish rally*, I thought, having looked to one then the other as if watching a heated table-tennis match.

"I wasn't aware Go-mi had a stepmother. She is always such a bright and cheerful girl," my teacher offered. At that, my stepmom frowned and furrowed her brow deeply, which instantly put ten years on her face.

"Her? Bright and cheerful?"

"Well, yes, she doesn't have any particularly close friends but she's so sunny and sweet that…"

"Sunny? Her? Hah, that'd make a dog laugh," my stepmom shot back. Both my teacher and I jumped and turned to her.

"I don't know what her behavior is like at school," my stepmom continued. "But you know what she's like at home?

She's cold and distant and terribly rude. She doesn't even acknowledge me, much less talk to me."

My teacher's face went hard. The sun was baking her head. I could see a circular patch of sweat that had bloomed in the front of her blouse. I realized I hadn't stood in the sun like that ever since I'd become translucent. I wondered what would happen if I did. Would I melt? Would I disappear? If only.

"She's always been like that," my stepmother continued. "She would ignore me with that innocent look on her face. I tried to be understanding, telling myself she's still young, that she's scared of my eye. But it's been years! That mean little bitch. I tried to be nice to her but she wouldn't let me and would only glare at me with hate in her eyes. After her father died, I had to slave away to pay for bills and food and her allowance, all for what? What thanks do I get? That little bitch. I'm glad I haven't had to see her the last few days."

After vomiting up this torrent of words, she became winded and short of breath. My teacher took half a step back, her face pale.

"Ma'am... Are you sure Go-mi is at her grandmother's?"

Just then, I quietly slipped away past my teacher and escaped through the front door.

Once out in the sun, I looked down at my body and saw that it was shimmering like light dancing on the surface of water as seen from the bottom of the pool. I didn't melt or disappear. I was beautiful. I lifted my hand up and turned it around slowly, admiring myself. I saw my teacher leave, marching down the corridor. My stepmother was yelling after her, "She's not the only one without parents, you know! I don't have any parents either! I'm an orphan too!"

Where should I go?

I hadn't been outside in days, but there was nowhere I wanted to go to and no place that needed me. So I began to walk. I should be at my extracurricular class right now, so it was refreshing to be outdoors for once. The feeling didn't last, however, as I was soon overwhelmed by an overpowering fatigue. It must have been the noise. The sounds of traffic, of people talking, and of birds chattering vibrated through me in waves, causing wave after wave of powerful nausea. After only a few steps, I crumpled to a heap near a storefront.

What am I going to do?

In movies, people who have turned invisible do exciting things like rob a bank or become a spy or secretly follow their lover around town, but I wasn't interested in money and didn't have any friends, much less a boyfriend. Besides, I wasn't sure I could rob a bank when I couldn't pass through any safes or walls. What was I to do? What did I *want* to do? I sat there on the steps and thought for a long time.

I concluded that I wanted to go to a place far away from here.

But where?

I'd been presented with the opportunity to quite literally go anywhere I wanted but couldn't think of a single place. Damn, my life is so boring. The past thirteen years was a joke. I sat there like Rodin's *The Thinker*, bemoaning my own fate. But it was too late for regrets, and even if I were given a second chance to return to my non-translucent state and live a life worth living, I wasn't sure I was up for the challenge. I decided to stop thinking these useless thoughts. Instead, I sat and people-watched. I tried talking to a few of them. *Hey, kid, you headed to taekwondo lessons? Ma'am, I see you bought some green onions. They're quite sweet this time of year. Sir, how was your hike up the mountain? Ma'am, where's your umbrella? It's supposed to rain tonight*. The people passed by silently, and I felt slighted somehow. I grew bored of this game. In the end, I simply sat there with nothing to do and nowhere to go until darkness fell. The shops around me shut down and the foot traffic slowed. Where did everyone go? They must have gone home. Home, where it's warm and inviting, where they can rest with their loved ones. I became jealous of the people hurrying home, jealous to the point I felt a sharp twinge at the end of my nose. I leaped to my feet but remained fixed to the spot. If there was a place I wanted to go, I would have trudged endlessly forth until I reached that destination. But there was no such place.

There were almost no people around at this hour. The last bus of the day pulled up at the bus stop. I watched as the night-shift employee at the nearby convenience store relieved his colleague, shrugging into his work vest and going around to the back of the counter. Then I headed home. A slightly damp night wind, possibly hinting at rain to come, kept pushing me in the direction of the tailwind. Humming softly to myself—*don't wanna go, don't wanna go*—I took slow, measured steps toward home.

It was past midnight by the time I arrived, and I assumed I'd have to wait by the door until it was opened. But when I got off the elevator on our floor, I noticed there was an apartment with its front door slightly ajar, causing light to flood out into the outdoor corridor. Upon closer inspection, I saw it was ours. I heard a man's unfamiliar voice booming out into the hallway. Surprised, I withdrew into myself. I could tell the voice was angry. There was a fight going on.

I squeezed through the crack in the door and into the apartment, where I was greeted by complete and utter chaos. Food was strewn on the floor of the kitchen. Broken plates and bowls were littered everywhere. One of the chairs had its leg broken and was toppled over on its side. No one could have possibly heard me coming, yet I tiptoed quietly past the front door to the living room, where things took a turn for the worse. The closets and drawers had all been opened and their contents turned over on the floor, as if a group of robbers had worked the place over in an incredible hurry. All our belongings were thrown carelessly across the floor. In the midst of it all sat my stepmother. She was without her eye patch, which she wore religiously even when she was home, and her hair was a mess. When I realized the reddish-brown splotch on her face was actually dried blood, I looked up at where she was glaring and saw a man standing there.

At first, I thought he was a high-school kid. He was barely a few inches taller than me and so thin that I couldn't believe he was a grown-up. But I saw I was wrong. The man may have been of slight build, but he had the face of an adult man, and in fact looked much older than my stepmother. His small, beady eyes and the ugly wrinkles spreading outward from his flat nose gave away his age. Those were the sorts of wrinkles that plagued the faces of people who spent their whole lives frowning. Frowning and screaming at others who are even more powerless. That is the kind of spite that ages the abuser, not the victim. The kind of spite that etches itself deeply in their faces.

I knew of one other man with that sort of face. My late father, who had spent his years screaming at my mother first, then my stepmother, always demanding and asking something of them. Although this stranger's build and sense of style were nothing like my father's, there was something about him that was similar. It was clear what his relationship was with my stepmom. There was only one explanation for why she was on the floor and he was towering over her, both glaring at each other with hate. I spent my whole childhood witnessing the same dynamic. *What a terrible fate this woman has*, I thought. I don't know if she had always been this unlucky or if she had brought this on herself, but damn. Suddenly, the man plopped down on the couch. He then reached into his pants pocket and took out a lighter and a cigarette, which he proceeded to light.

"Put that out," my stepmother muttered. She was still glaring at him as if to kill him. But she wasn't posing much of a threat. In fact, the more her right eye twisted and glared at the man, the more pronounced her swollen, squashed left eyelid became.

"I said, put that out."

The man shot her a look, then rubbed the cigarette out crudely on the arm of the couch. He then bared his teeth, causing the cigarette smoke to seep out down his chin. Instantly, I sensed what was coming next. But before I had the chance to look away, the man reached out and grabbed my stepmom's hair. At the same time, he coiled his other hand back like a lithe snake and slapped her hard in the face.

I squeezed my eyes shut but could still feel the pain. The rough skin of his palm slamming against her cheek with an ear-splitting sound. The white burst of light that renders you senseless. The despair that comes from knowing you can never go back to the smooth, unbroken world you used to know. The searing hatred that fills you up from the edges of your toes. I felt heat rushing to my face, though my body had no sense of temperature or breath. I exhaled. I saw my stepmother curled on the floor clutching her cheek and thought I was looking at myself.

She sat there for a while, not moving. In the harsh glare of the fluorescent lights, I saw heavy, dark bruises on her legs. Staring at those bruises, I felt something bubbling up in the pit of my stomach. This wasn't the first time I'd seen my stepmother getting beaten up, and I myself had endured my share of such beatings. In fact, I had seen this scene played out so many times that I was sick and tired of it. Yet each time this happened, it felt new despite it being so familiar, causing a fresh wave of pain. Just as I was thinking that, the man suddenly turned and grabbed his jacket from the couch. Roughly, he stuffed his arms into the sleeves. Then he stomped to the front door. As he did, he kicked at the plates and other broken bits of our belongings. He pushed open the door and left. At the sound, my stepmother started where she sat and looked up. Her nose was bleeding and her entire face was a bloody pulp.

Painfully, she sat up. She glanced around at the mess in the living room and the kitchen, before her gaze fell upon the front door through which the stranger had left. There was no further movement, although we could hear the soft, rumbling sounds of thunder from far away. I could tell what she was thinking. I used to wish the same thing. Every time my father stormed out of the house after beating me, my mother, or my stepmother, I used to wish the same thing.

That no one would walk through those doors again.

So that I could be alone.

My stepmother sat there for a long time, staring at the front door. But I knew. I knew the man wouldn't return. He wouldn't even call her. He will try to forget her, spitting at her memory, calling her a miserable, unlucky bitch. And, in fact, he will forget. He'll go on with his life as if he'd never even known her. Perhaps my stepmother realized that, too. She finally lifted her gaze off the front door and fixed it on one spot in the distance. I tried to see where she was looking at but there was nothing there. I stood there, blinking, and watched as my stepmom slowly began bowing down, head first, on the floor. Bringing her arms and legs close to her body, she stayed there in a crouching pose.

And then, she slowly turned translucent.

The translucence began somewhere in the center of her body and quickly spread outward, as if someone had pressed a button and snapped her body back. Her see-through body was now revealing the dark streaks in the linoleum left there a long time ago by a heating iron. Not knowing what to do, I stood there and watched the process unfold. Time slowed to a crawl.

Even after she had turned fully translucent, my stepmother didn't get up from where she was. She must not be aware of what had happened. Neither was I, at first. *Maybe she was dead?* I shuddered at the thought and opened my mouth to call out to her, not knowing whether or not she could hear me. What did I used to call her? I was ready to call out to her, but I couldn't remember what I used to call her. We may not have been fond of each other, but we had lived under the same roof for many years. I must have called her by something, but I couldn't remember what. After a long while, I managed to mutter, "Hey…"

Startled, she turned around and looked up at me. Our eyes met.

She was not looking somewhere past me but directly into my eyes. I was also meeting her gaze full on, not just her one good eye but the left eye that she had lost in the childhood accident. We remained there, staring at each other. The fluorescent lights were filtering through her face, which was still etched with the handprints of the man who had slapped her. But her face was no longer hard to look at. Instead it inspired a bit of pity. *She does have a rather unlucky-looking face*, I thought to myself. She reminded me of the character actor known for always playing the role of a downtrodden, poverty-stricken mother. With that, I let her lay it on me as much as she wanted.

"How long have you been standing there?"

"From the beginning."

"What do you mean, from the beginning?"

"From the time I went missing."

"You were always in that condition?"

"Always in this condition."

After this strange back and forth, we ran out of things to say.

We sat there surrounded by the unholy mess of the living room. I felt embarrassed and awkward. But it also felt like déjà vu, as if we'd been through this sort of situation before. A time when she and I had sat there, swollen and silenced like a pair of ugly still-life paintings. It was after my father had torn the whole place up then beat us for having tried to stop him before storming out of the house. It had been late at night, the house filled with broken and shattered things, with us left feeling miserable and desperate. Not unlike tonight. It was a different abuser this time, but always the same things are broken. What did we do that last time? I remember sitting dazed and feeling lost for quite some time. Then we got up to clear away the broken things. We threw away the things that were completely broken, and mended the things that still had a chance. We weren't close enough to confide in each other and share our wounded feelings, so we went through the whole process in complete silence.

As I was reminiscing, my stepmom got up and slowly walked towards the bathroom. She must want to see herself in the mirror as I had. She'll receive quite a shock at the sight of herself. She was gone for a long time. When she came back, however, she didn't look like she'd received a bad fright. She looked rather pleased, as if she were enjoying herself. It felt bittersweet. I must have worn that exact same lighthearted expression the second I realized I no longer bore any responsibility for anyone or anything, that I no longer had to reveal myself to anyone, that it was all finally *over*, and I was as free as a soldier who had just heard the trumpets announcing a ceasefire. Why is it always the same with people like us? My stepmom tottered over to me and asked, "Are we dead?"

"I don't think so, but maybe, yeah."

"What kind of answer is that?"

"I'm not sure, actually. I've only been like this a few days."

She stared at me, her face still badly swollen, then broke into a small grin. *Does she think we're friends now?* I turned my face away from her. But I, too, had a smile on my face. Worried she might catch me smiling from behind, as my head was completely see-through, I quickly arranged my face into a blank expression, but it was too late. Being see-through means anyone can see through your lies, too. Oh well. I decided to laugh it off. It wasn't easy, but it also wasn't hard.

"I don't feel sleepy or hungry," I said.

"Me, neither. I don't feel any pain."

"But you can't use any of your strength, either. You can't use any force."

"My goodness, you're right!"

"See what I mean?"

"Yes."

My stepmother was by the front door, struggling with the horseshoe-shaped doorstop that was keeping the door open. She was trying to remove it to close the door but failed. Since neither of us could open or shut the door with any ease, it might have made better sense to keep it open. But that would mean the neighbors would see the place when they walked by and witness the mess inside. *Who cares? They wouldn't be able to see us.* My stepmom must have come to the same conclusion for she soon gave up trying to close the door and returned to the living room.

"Listen," she said, while lying in a heap. "Were you here, in the house, that day?"

"What day?"

"Last Saturday."

What happened last Saturday? I wondered. I'd long lost any sense of time, so I had to reach back in my memory. Then I remembered. It was the day my homeroom teacher came to check up on me.

"Yes," I said.

"...I see."

"Why do you ask?"

Even before the words were out of my mouth, I realized why she had asked. When I saw her lips start to quiver, I leaped up as if someone had stabbed me with something sharp.

"No, please don't start with that!"

I could tell what she was going to say. I was sure of it. It was as if I'd already heard it. But I didn't want to hear it. She was going to start apologizing, ask for forgiveness, or defensively talk about how difficult her own life had been. Empty, useless talk. Words that couldn't change anything but somehow gave the sensation they made everything better. Words that became emptier and more disgusting the more you mulled them over. If she were to say any of those things to me, I knew I'd explode. I regretted letting her see me smile. Does she think everything's okay between us because we had that small moment? It's always so easy and simple with these people. They destroy and destroy, then leave and never look back. I felt small air bubbles pushing up from somewhere deep inside me. I wished I could explode. Explode into a thousand translucent pieces so that I could never be rearranged back into human form.

Staggering, I pushed my way towards the door. My stepmother looked up at me in alarm. I was going to leave. Disappear. I'll leave this place and never come back. Never even think about it. I didn't know what I had to do to disappear, but I was planning to do everything I possibly could.

The front door was drawing closer. Heavy rain was pelting the world outside.

Suddenly, something big and brown fluttered in and landed on my shoulder. It was a moth the size of my palm. I screamed and stood there frozen to the spot. My stepmother came running. She also screamed when she saw the moth but soon sprang into action, slapping the moth away. It fluttered up and latched onto the ceiling. Although it was gone, we both stood there rooted to the spot.

In that moment, I knew I would carry that sensation with me forever and remember it more clearly than anything else for the rest of my life. The feeling of her hand making contact with my body, when her translucent body joined mine before latching off. In that brief moment, she and I had become one before breaking off again. Much like how two drops of water merge, then divide into two again. I knew a part of her hand was still a part of my shoulder and that a part of my shoulder was now one with her hand. I knew we were both thinking the same thing. No one and nothing could separate us from each other.

From far away came distant sounds of thunder that rolled gently past us. The rain was becoming torrential. From the crack in the door, we could glimpse the world outside, filled with long shards of rain illuminated at times by bursts of lightning. We saw rainwater pooling along the outdoor hallway. Soon, it would flow into our apartment.

I don't recall which one of us made the first move. But, after giving each other a knowing look, we moved toward the front door and began pushing at the horseshoe-shaped doorstop with all our might. We had to use every ounce of strength but we managed to lift it slightly off the ground. As it budged, the strong winds blew the door shut, and the resulting force sent us bowling backwards. If we had our old bodies, we'd have received quite a blow to our heads, if not a concussion, but because we were both soft, jelly forms by now, we were merely pancaked on the floor, staring up at the ceiling.

The world became silent.

Lying there, I turned my head to look at the front door, which was now closed. All we did was close one door, but it was enough to block out all the sounds and noises from the world outside. It was odd how the silence felt. It was profound, as if we'd muted all sound. It felt as if nothing bad could happen to us anymore. Gazing at my stepmother sprawled out across my old sneakers, I heaved a deep sigh. *If I'm going to lie here, might as well get comfortable.* With that, I closed my eyes.

"Everything's so flat," I murmured.

The floor was flat against our backs. So was the world it was connected to. I was lying there like quivering jelly without flowing to one side or pooling in a puddle somewhere. Someone could try to push me, but I'd remain faithfully here in this solidly flat world. We lay there each in our own way, and we could lie there until we wanted to get up, until there was a place we wanted to go. We could stay here as long as we wanted, round and flat, in this silent, gentle state.

With my eyes closed, I pressed my back more tightly against the floor. Outside, the rain was not slowing down.

Strong winds were carrying the tides of rain, spreading them far and wide across our world. But with our front door shut, none of the rain would make it into our house. It no longer mattered that it was raining outside.

IGUANA AND ME

He's really gone, I murmured to myself. Only after I'd voiced the words did the anger slowly creep up inside me, but whether the feeling was anger or something else I wasn't sure.

I slipped off my shoes and walked into the apartment. The sun was setting, casting an orange glow across the room and the empty places where his belongings had been. What a pretty setting for a post-breakup scene, and how befitting. Except for that *thing* he left behind.

The desk, cleared of Je-ho's things, was sparse and quiet save for a glass terrarium perched on its surface. I drew near and peeked over the plastic lid. I hoped for a second that maybe Je-ho had taken the thing with him, leaving behind an empty terrarium, but of course I was wrong, of course I locked eyes with it as it lay lounging on the piece of decorative wood inside. Locked eyes with Je-ho's iguana.

We glared at each other for a long time. I was the one doing the glaring, and the iguana was simply looking at me as it lay splayed out like an ugly rubber toy. I glared at his fingernail-shaped eyes and its triangular head, the spines sticking out of its backbone and its long, spindly tail. I was getting exhausted. What was I hoping to achieve? Glaring wasn't going to help. Feeling tired and helpless, I plopped down on the bed and realized something was missing. The thin fleece comforter I kept on my bed. It was gone. Je-ho must have taken it. Since he was the one who had bought it last winter, I couldn't accuse him of stealing. Strictly speaking, he hadn't.

I sat there, on my now fleece-less bed, and stared at the iguana. That bastard.

I had known all along that if Je-ho and I were ever to break up and he took his things and left, he would leave the iguana behind.

I first had this ominous foreboding the day he moved in. Moving in together wasn't a grand, formal affair. Je-ho simply came to live in my rented apartment. When I heard his lease was expiring, I begged Je-ho to move in with me and, after some hesitation, he ultimately gave in. At the time, I was hopelessly in love with him. I couldn't believe the love of my life was becoming my roommate. So smitten was I that when I saw the glass terrarium among the rest of his things, all I did was point to it and ask what it was. Frowning, Je-ho replied, "It's an iguana?" As if having an iguana among your everyday belongings was the most ordinary thing ever. Not knowing what to say, I bent down to look inside. In doing so, I caught a strong whiff of a fishy odor mixed with the smell of rotting meat. Algae was growing in all four corners of the terrarium. Clearly, this thing hadn't been cleaned in a while. Holding my breath, I studied the inside of the glass case until my gaze finally fell upon an iguana hunkered beneath a rotten piece of wood. It was maybe about forty to fifty centimeters long, inclusive of its tail, with a greenish, bumpy, patchy hide reminiscent of chicken skin, and legs too short for its body. Was Je-ho planning on keeping this disgusting thing here, in our house? I turned to ask and saw that he had his back turned to me as he rummaged in his things. His back, hunched over and determined, seemed resolute somehow. Looking back and forth at the terrarium then at Je-ho's back, I changed my mind and asked instead, "So, what's his name?"

Still with his back turned to me, Je-ho responded curtly, "He doesn't have a name. It's just an iguana."

"Just Iguana then?" I asked. But Je-ho didn't turn around. He continued removing his things from the boxes. I stared blankly at him for a while, then, lifting the terrarium, placed it on one corner of the desk.

It goes without saying the iguana had caused some discomfort—not a whole lot, but still a noticeable amount of discomfort—in what I assumed was going to be a happy relationship between Je-ho and me. For one thing, the terrarium was too big and bulky for our already cramped apartment, and it stank up the entire place when not cleaned regularly. Someone had to chop up vegetables and place clean water for the iguana to drink and look in on it from time to time to see if it was still alive. Je-ho did none of these things. Instead, he behaved as if the creature was an ugly eyesore and refused to even go near it. This meant that I was charged with the upkeep of the animal. And yet, as the seasons changed, I stupidly did not bring up the subject of the iguana with him. Most people in my position would have complained about the situation at least once or twice. But I didn't think complaining was going to change anything, and, to be completely honest, I didn't want to say anything to upset my boyfriend.

So it happened that a long time passed before I got to know the story behind the iguana. One evening, after dinner, the topic of our conversation turned to our past romantic relationships. Je-ho was on a passionate tirade against one of his former girlfriends when he suddenly pointed at the iguana and shouted, "That thing, do you know what happened with me and that thing?"

The story went like this. The iguana used to belong to Je-ho's ex-girlfriend. She had moved into Je-ho's old studio, where they were to shack up for a few months. The woman had brought the iguana along with the rest of her things. She explained to a surprised Je-ho that the reptile used to belong to her ex-boyfriend and that he had left it with her upon their breakup. According to Je-ho, she then went on screaming about her jerk ex-boyfriend who left her to go to Italy and learn how to become a barista. This preposterous story was enough to silence Je-ho, who decided not to fight her on the subject of the iguana, which meant that the iguana got to stay with them.

The two stayed together for a while, until the day they had a huge fight. The next day, after Je-ho returned from his part-time job, it had happened. The apartment was empty of her things, save for the terrarium and its occupant. Not one to stand for this nonsense, Je-ho immediately called up his ex and demanded she come pick up the iguana, but all he heard was, "I don't give a shit about the iguana. Give it to someone else or throw it away for all I care." Je-ho did a pretty good job mimicking a girly, bored voice as he repeated this story. Then, gritting his teeth angrily, he muttered, "How was I supposed to throw away a living creature?"

Smiling, I stroked the back of his hand as he told me the story, but deep inside I knew. The two stories were surprisingly similar, and I sensed that, one day, Je-ho too would leave the iguana when he left me for good. But instead of doing something about this red flag, I changed the subject.

"So, how long do iguanas live anyway?"

At that, Je-ho calmed down and thought. "I don't know. Maybe five years? Ten?"

Meanwhile, the iguana lay stretched out inside the terrarium like a dead piece of bark, looking as if it couldn't hear or comprehend anything, and even if it could, that whatever was going on had nothing to do with him.

"Maybe one of our club members can adopt him?" suggested Eugene when I told her the story. Then she turned around so I could zip up her suit. I grabbed the long zipper attached to the back of her instructor-grade wetsuit. Would anyone want to adopt something as gross as an iguana? I wondered. But maybe Eugene was right. One of the pool's members might be up for it. Maybe one of the middle-aged women who came for the afternoon water aerobics lessons? One of them might want to adopt a pet iguana for her kids. I pictured the faces of each of my students before turning my back to Eugene. She grimaced as she zippered me up.

"I'll do the warm-ups today. Get some rest. You look like shit." After giving both my shoulders a short squeeze, Eugene marched out to the pool. Soon I heard the low bellow of her whistle. I sat and studied my reflection in the opposite mirror. I did look like shit. My eyes were swollen, my cheeks wan and grey. I looked like someone had stretched a badly textured patch of leather over a mess of bones. Wait a minute. Now I see what I looked like. An iguana. As soon as I realized that, I leaped up as if caught in flames. Lifting one leg on a bench, I began rubbing at my thighs and calves to reduce the swelling. I pressed and rubbed until I heard the long wail of Eugene's whistle. I didn't feel any better.

Before heading home for the day, I stuck a flyer advertising *Free Iguana, Inquire at Registration Desk* on the wall of the swimming pool. I waited a few days but no one called.

This meant that when I went home in the afternoon, the iguana was there. I couldn't leave it to die, which meant I had to feed it. I didn't want it to stink, which meant I had to clean the terrarium from time to time, still in shock and disbelief at how this had happened. Given the tiny size of the apartment, the terrarium came into view no matter where I was—whether I was eating dinner or hanging the laundry out to dry. At night, I lay on my side and stared at the darkened terrarium before I fell asleep.

Several times, I leaped out of bed and grabbed my phone, intending to call Je-ho. Just as he had done, and as his ex-girlfriend, or rather his ex-ex-girlfriend had done, I had half a mind to yell at him to take the iguana back. But before I could press the call button, I realized I wasn't sure what to say or how to begin saying it. So I gave up. I knew what Je-ho was going to say. And just as he had been made speechless at what his ex-ex-girlfriend had said, I knew I was going to be rendered speechless by him. I'd regret having called him in the first place. And what if he mistook the call as a sign that I was still into him? What if he thought I was using the iguana as a pretense to call him? I'd rather be a slave to the stupid iguana for the rest of my life than let him think that. Then I rubbed my face in frustration against the new comforter I bought before falling asleep.

Several months passed. One Friday, I had a few drinks with Eugene after work. Since the next day was the weekend, we decided to get drunk, but it turned out there weren't many bars in this part of town. We ended up in the same bar Je-ho and I used to frequent, so talk naturally turned to the subject of my ex-boyfriend. I poured a shot of soju into a big mug of beer, then, stirring it with a chopstick, went into a long rant about Je-ho. How he used to play those loud, annoying games on his phone late into the night. How he would sit and wait without lifting a finger until I'd set the table and get the food ready every time we ordered take-out. How he would keep wads of tissue in his pants pockets for some reason, so that every time I did the laundry, the washing machine would turn into a real mess. What else? What other stupid things did he do? I chatted as my mind raced with more things to gripe about Je-ho, when Eugene, after having listened quietly all this time, finally spoke.

"So why did you go out with him in the first place?"

I would have been less taken aback if she had screamed insults at me or stormed off. Swallowing, I stared blankly at Eugene. The look of sincere curiosity on her face was even more sobering. Seeing my expression harden, Eugene quickly followed up. "I mean, we're not getting any younger. How long are you going to let these fuckboys mess with you? I'm saying this because I care."

And it looked like she really did care. "Yeah, I know, right?" I said. "Why did I date such a loser? Next time, I have to find a better one."

With that, I tossed back my drink and poured myself another soju-and-beer cocktail.

Back home, with no one to watch or judge, I removed my clothes and stripped down to my panties before lying spread-eagled on the cold floor. I felt something rising up inside my chest, somewhere deep past my throat. It wasn't sadness or anger. What was it? What was this feeling? Staring up at the ceiling, I realized that I was feeling miserable. I sat bolt upright. This brought me completely eye-level with the iguana that had been staring at me through the glass wall of its terrarium. He was watching me as if I were the animal inside a cage, and the thought made me grin.

"What are you looking at? We've both been abandoned, you and me," I said. "Abandoned by that loser. For real though. I'm not saying this because I'm drunk. That jerk left us both."

As I said these words, the iguana stared up at me with its golden eyes wide open. Suddenly, feeling a surge of courage, I reached past the plastic lid into the terrarium. Whenever I cleaned out the cage, I would do so gingerly, taking care to stay far away from the iguana as I swiped at the algae growing on the sides of the wall, but being shit-faced drunk had taken away all inhibition. I reached in to touch the iguana.

I thought it might run away terrified, but I was wrong. My fingers made contact with the flat area between the creature's eyes (its forehead?). Its skin was smooth and soft, nothing like the coarse, rough surface I'd imagined from its bumpy scales. Beneath the silky hide, I could feel the bones of its skull. With two fingers, I slowly stroked the iguana. It lifted its head and closed its eyes. The iguana remained there in that position. I wasn't sure whether he liked the sensation or hated it, but, as he did not bite or claw at my fingers, I continued stroking the lizard. It's a living creature, I thought.

Just then, I heard a low, quiet voice from somewhere below my fingers.

"Um, excuse me."

I leaped back in horror, mouth twisted in a silent scream. I pulled my hand back and used both arms to cover myself up. I looked around but of course no one was there. Was I hallucinating? Maybe the sound was coming from the neighbors? Terrified, my mind raced with every other possibility I could think of for where the voice had come from, but then I heard the sound of something knocking. I looked down and saw the iguana knocking against the terrarium wall with its foot. When our eyes met, the iguana spoke.

"I'm very sorry for asking you this, but… Do you think you can teach me how to swim?"

"How to what?"

Only after answering his question did I realize, absurdly, that I was talking to an iguana.

When our eyes met again, the iguana gently squeezed one of its eyes closed then opened it again. It was the sort of apologetic expression one might make after having inconvenienced someone despite their very best of intentions, and this knowledge made the whole experience seem so much more absurd and surreal that I dashed around, frantically picking up my clothes and throwing them back on again, muttering to myself as I did so.

I had a lot of questions, but now that I was sitting across from the iguana, I couldn't find the words. Literally. I wasn't sure if I had to address him in the polite way, using honorifics, or talk casually to him the way I would to a peer. It didn't feel right to use honorifics toward a creature that was most definitely younger than I was, but it similarly felt rude to talk down to him as if he were an old friend. I went for something in between.

"So um... Would you care for a drink as we..."

"I'd like some water, thank you."

I headed to the kitchen and brought back a shallow bowl full of cold water. Bowing low, the iguana began drinking the water. I didn't know what to think. The iguana must have guessed as much. After a long while, it spoke.

"This must have come as a surprise to you," it said in the slow, measured voice of a precocious child.

"I mean, I was surprised, yeah... Er, can you explain what's going on...?"

I responded in a tone that could either be read as respectful or casual. As if gathering its thoughts, the iguana stared out into space then drank some more water. Wiping its mouth with its foot, the lizard began calmly.

"I'd be happy to answer any questions you have."

He's smart, I thought, then rushed to ask the most burning question.

"When did you learn to talk like that? I mean, talk to humans?"

I blushed as I asked the question. Je-ho and I had kept the animal for a year and a half, and I'd cared for him for months after Je-ho and I broke up. That meant I'd lived with the iguana for two years. Never had I thought I needed to be mindful of the attention of a reptilian pet, so there were many times I engaged in wild, rather questionable behavior in his presence.

"I learned a long time ago. But don't worry, I didn't see or hear anything," the iguana rushed to add, as if reading my thoughts. Obviously, this meant that he *had* seen and heard quite a few things.

"So um… Why did you feel the need to suddenly speak up now? Today?" I didn't ask the question I most wanted to ask, which was: *Why me?*

"I believe I am dying. Before I die, there's something I'd like to do."

"You're dying? How?"

"Would you understand if I told you I haven't received proper enough care? I've gone a long time without access to sunlight or adequate nutrition. I've managed to cling on this far, but now I feel I've reached the end. Just so you know, I'm not accusing you of anything. I know what your situation is like. Look at my tail. My last shed didn't go so well."

With that, the iguana turned around so I could examine its tail which was a sad, broken-off stub. I couldn't believe I hadn't noticed that wound. In fact, this was the first time I'd studied the lizard in the light. It appeared that his tail wasn't the only issue. He was blotched and bruised all over and clearly suffered from ill health. I was struck by an overpowering sense of shame and guilt.

"Anyway, I don't think I'll last many more months. I'm not scared of dying, but there's something I really wanted to do before I go. I wasn't sure how to bring it up, but when you came up to me earlier and spoke to me, stroked me, I thought I might as well go for it. After all, whether I die in this tank or get sold to the circus as a talking iguana, it's all the same to me."

As he spoke of getting sold to the circus, the iguana looked up at me pleadingly, as if begging me not to even think of doing such a thing. Instead of replying, I asked another question.

"What is it you want?"

At that, the iguana sat up straight as if he'd been waiting for this moment. He answered without a moment's hesitation.

"I want to go to Mexico. I'll first have to learn how to swim though, if I want to get there."

What?

I opened my mouth to speak but not finding the right words, closed it again. His dream was so hopelessly ridiculous that I didn't know how to begin telling him so, but I had also heard the determination in his voice and stance. This was a decision he'd reached after much careful consideration. It was the kind of decision no one could talk him out of.

The iguana stared at me with his golden-brown eyes. Like a guilty criminal, I avoided his gaze. I was still confused over what was happening. Deep down, I knew I'd just become involved in a major pain in the ass.

The iguana refused my proposal to take him to Mexico myself. He insisted I would already be doing him a huge favor by teaching him how to swim, and besides, he wanted to do it on his own. After a long argument with the increasingly stubborn iguana, we agreed that I was to accompany him to a beach somewhere on the East Sea coast on the day of his departure. I wasn't happy with this arrangement.

"Do you realize how far away Mexico is? How would you even get there by yourself?"

I plopped the iguana down on my desk and brought up Google Maps on my computer. I chose somewhere off the coast of the East Sea as the starting point and a beach in Mexico as the destination. The distance was 11,500 kilometers.

"You see that? That's the distance between Seoul and Busan, multiplied seventeen times!"

The iguana merely sat there staring at the screen as if it contained a secret to swimming the best way from here to Mexico. I felt my heart grow soft.

"Does it have to be Mexico? I heard Hawaii's also great. Or what about Bali?"

I assumed he simply wanted to spend the rest of his life sunning on a warm tropical beach somewhere. But the iguana shook his head firmly.

"If it's not Mexico, the whole trip would be meaningless."

"Why? What's in Mexico?"

"Iguana heaven."

"What?"

I thought I heard him correctly the first time, but I had to ask. The iguana explained.

"Iguana heaven. It's a place filled with fresh grass, saltwater beaches, and freshwater pools all year long. No iguana ever goes hungry. During the day, they lie underneath the sun and rest. Or they go for walks across the warm, sunbaked rocks. At night, they find a cozy spot in between a couple of bigger rocks and go to sleep, lulled by the sound of the waves."

He continued in a dreamy tone. "If I could live there for just one day, I know I'll die happy."

"Who told you about that place?"

"My mother. After I was hatched, I spent a few months with her as she took care of me. That's when she taught me the human language. Mother told me those amazing stories of Mexico, but she didn't tell me to go there. She must have thought it was impossible. I later learned that I was born in a pet shop specializing in reptiles. Mother was also born and bred there, so she likely never made it to Mexico, either."

The iguana reached out and placed one of its feet over my hand. "And I wouldn't have dreamed of going there either, if it weren't for you. Thank you very much."

I hadn't agreed to anything yet, so I couldn't help but smile as I met his gaze. I guess I could teach him how to swim. After all, I was a swimming instructor. But I wasn't sure whether letting him swim out to sea would be a responsible thing to do, even if he had mastered how to swim. He's going to sink. He wouldn't make it past the oceans of Korea, much less get to Mexico. I couldn't voice the words that were swirling around my head, so I simply stroked his feet.

The iguana wanted to begin lessons right away but there were no pools I could take him to, for obvious reasons. In the end, I decided on using one of those big rubber tubs people use to make kimchi in. I bought the biggest tub I could find from the local hardware shop. After filling the red tub with water and placing the iguana inside where it still smelled strongly of rubber, I saw that it was a good enough size.

We began our first lesson the day I bought the tub. I taught him how to kick as he needed to gain strength in his legs first. He learned how to use his tail to change direction and how to go limp and float on the surface when he was too tired to swim. Grabbing each of his hind legs in my hands, I swung them up and down, demonstrating how to kick. The iguana relaxed in my hands as he tried to take in the movement, then when I let go, tried to do as he was told. *Good, good!* I urged him on. *Breathe! Lift your head! Good!*

There was more to do than just the swimming lessons. The iguana had to be placed on a strict diet regimen, rich in fresh vegetables like bok choy, kale, and endives along with vitamin-infused iguana pellets and calcium powder. Once he was full, I made him take fifty laps around the room to help him digest the food and improve his fundamentals. The iguana ate whatever I gave him and did as he was told. Even when it looked like he was close to giving up, he would invariably force himself to his feet and finish the lap. Seeing his determination, I was filled with a sense of hope. Perhaps, if he were lucky and the gods of the sky and earth smiled at him—or maybe he should be leaning on the god of the seas—but in any case, if everything were to go in his favor, then maybe, just maybe, he might make it to Mexico. I knew the possibilities were slim to none, but I still pictured him sometimes, exhausted and scrawny, taking his first few steps on Mexican soil.

I don't know when it began, but we started sleeping together in my bed. Before this, I had no idea that iguanas loved soft, plushy things, as opposed to their own scaly, dry skin. The iguana would lie flat on the pillow next to mine, chatting nonstop before finally falling asleep.

One night, the talk turned to Je-ho. When I mentioned how he took my fleece blanket after the breakup, the iguana smiled in the dark. I'd meant the story to be funny but seeing him smile irked me somehow. As I lay there pouting, the iguana explained, "His ex-ex-girlfriend was the same way. She took all his things with him but left me behind."

Rendered speechless, I stroked the iguana's little stub of a tail. Smiling, he continued. "Humans are quick learners. That's your greatest advantage."

Rubbing his tail against my wrist, he slowly closed his eyes. I grinned. The iguana clearly had picked up on social manners. Stroking the now fast asleep iguana's forehead, I realized I was actually getting fond of this crusty creature. Why couldn't we stay roommates? We have plenty of sun here. Korea may not be Mexico, but our summers are known to be hot. I imagined us out for a walk in the sun with the iguana on a leash. It made me grin. I'd been sleeping better and waking up more refreshed lately.

Eugene glared at me and didn't say a word. She didn't have to, as her glare spoke plenty. Like, *I knew you were weird, but I didn't take you for a psycho*. I would have thought the same if I were in her situation. If Eugene had told me she was in the midst of teaching her talking poodle how to swim, I'd think she'd gone insane, too.

"I didn't ask you here so we could dick around," Eugene curtly broke the silence, swirling her iced coffee with her straw. *I wasn't dicking around*, I was about to insist but kept my mouth shut when I realized this wasn't that kind of conversation. We were sitting at the café in the same building as the swimming pool. After we clocked out, Eugene asked to talk, mentioning that she had something important to say. Something was up. Taking a long sip of her coffee, Eugene looked up at me.

"I'm only here till next week. I've put in my notice."

I had guessed this was what she was going to say. It turned out my guess was correct. Eugene had been behaving strangely the past few days, so I wasn't surprised. She'd been coming late to work and instead of closely attending to her students, made them take constant laps around the pool. I myself had been preoccupied with the iguana and our private swimming lessons, but even I thought Eugene had been especially irresponsible. Now it turned out she had quit her job.

"What are you going to do?" I asked, not out of curiosity but rather as an act of courtesy towards a longtime work colleague.

Her eyes twinkling, Eugene gushed, "I got my Pilates certification. I'm going to open my own studio."

"What? Are you serious?"

"Yes! I actually got certified a while back. And I've secured a nice storefront not too far from here."

I had no idea Eugene had been training to become a Pilates instructor much less a certified one. And now she was opening her own Pilates studio.

"Honestly, I don't think there's a future in swimming. You have to shower and dry your hair after each swim and carry around wet, smelly clothes. You have to swim in a pool filled with strangers, with everyone ogling each other in their swimsuits. Who wants that? These days, people want to work out in style." Eugene spoke matter-of-factly as she sipped her coffee.

I sat there, listening with my mouth open. Her words were very persuasive. It must have been the air of authority bestowed by the certification. Only then did I realize that my classes had steadily dwindled the past few years whereas it seemed a new Pilates or yoga class was opening every other block. If I had to choose, I'd choose Pilates over swimming as well. I imagined Eugene sitting cross-legged on a yoga mat dressed in skin-tight Lycra, her arms gracefully stretched above her head. I didn't want to admit it but it made for a good image.

"You and I both majored in physical education. We didn't go to college so we could rot away in some local swim club. We have to find another path. You should, too. It's not too late."

Eugene was serious. Her advice wasn't anything revolutionary, but I nodded anyway. I truly believed she was right. At the same time, I couldn't help but wonder where she got the money to pay for the certification training and the down payment on the Pilates studio. She must have rich parents or be up to her neck in bank loans. As I was thinking that, I felt like I'd swallowed a mouthful of mud. I was disappointed at myself for thinking such nasty thoughts. I couldn't bear to face Eugene, so I kept my head bowed and bit down on my straw. I regretted having told her the story about the iguana.

I was still depressed after I'd come home, given the iguana his swimming lesson, and fed him his vegetables. In fact, the weight on my chest seemed to grow bigger. I kept biting down on my lower lip.

I used to think my life was fine. I wasn't making too much money but it wasn't like I was going under. Besides, I'd always loved to swim and I was good at it. This life wasn't too bad, all things considered. It wasn't necessarily a career I was going to devote my life to but I hadn't considered any other alternative. Upon hearing that a colleague had given up the same career option for something else entirely, however, a wave of fear and uncertainty washed over me, as if I'd realized the ground beneath my feet had given way and I was standing on a precipice. Can I keep going like this? Like a frog sitting oblivious inside a slowly heating pot, would I one day look back on my life and realize it was ruined with no chance of turning it back?

It wasn't like there was anything I could do in that moment. Days continued to pass regardless of my feelings. The pool hired a kid from college to replace Eugene. She had taken the job to make some money on the side during her break. I texted Eugene with the news on my way home, and she replied back several hours later. It was just an emoji, of a rabbit shrugging its shoulders and looking surprised.

The only times I was liberated from the depression and insecurity were the times I spent with the iguana. I had come up with a rigorous, specific schedule and pushed the iguana to train harder every day. In response, his swimming skills improved noticeably. I also began lowering the temperature incrementally every day, so now the creature was capable of swimming for hours in water as cold as ten degrees. He had even mastered the technique of sleeping while floating on the surface.

We headed to the Han River a couple of times during the wee hours when it was more likely no one else would be nearby. As the reptile swam across the river, I watched in fearful anticipation, ready to wade out there and fish him out if I had to, but each time, the iguana seemed to have no trouble reaching the other side of the riverbank. I waved when he turned around to look back at me, at which the iguana would jump back in the water and swim back. With my arms crossed, I watched as the iguana swam toward me with his head bobbing up and down, tracing a clean path in the river. I realized he would be leaving soon.

The days were getting hotter. It was obvious to the both of us that if he had to leave, he'd better leave at the height of summer when the water temperature was highest. If he missed this window, he'd have to wait another year.

More and more, the iguana asked me how good a swimmer I thought he was. When I said he was pretty good for an iguana but still needed work on a few skills, he stubbornly asked me what those were. As a result, I was forced to add more exercises to his swim plan to justify my claim with those exercises becoming increasingly far-fetched. Let's dangle a weight from your neck as you swim! Let's see how long you can stay underwater without breathing! Let's simulate different scenarios of having to escape various marine obstacles! What if a shark were to come after you? The iguana patiently carried out each wackadoodle idea, but even I knew I was fooling myself.

At night, as the iguana slept, I became lost in thought. Do I want him to leave? Or do I want him to stay? When I mulled over the question long enough, it soon became about me. What am I going to do with my life? Do I want to go on? Do I want to stop? What will happen to me if I keep going on? What will happen to me if I stop? These thoughts swirled in my head, getting neither deeper nor broader but simply growing harder and harder inside of me. I felt horrible but knew thinking wasn't going to change anything.

When the iguana finally announced that it was time, there was nothing I could say in return.

We arrived at Gyeongpodae at the East Sea before noon.

It was a bright, clear day, just as the weather report had forecast. There was not a cloud in the sky and the salty smell of the sea hung in the sun-warmed air. It was still early to be swimming at the beach, but, since it was the weekend, the beach was quite crowded. The scene looked pleasant enough, with people lazily walking in the sand in light summer clothing. Carrying a small fish tank containing the iguana, I looked for a deserted spot. Colorful mats and beach towels covered most of the beach. Maybe I shouldn't have chosen such a popular place. I had decided on this beach as it was just one train ride away. Unfortunately, I'd neglected to consider that if it was convenient for me, it would be convenient for everybody else. By the time I managed to locate a spot near end of the beach and lowered the fish tank on the sand, I was covered in sweat.

When I opened the lid, the iguana briskly trotted out. He gazed at the ocean before him with his four feet braced against the hot sand.

After a long beat, the iguana exclaimed softly, "Wow, this is much more amazing than I thought."

I'd half expected him to jump up and down in excitement, but he sounded calm and measured.

"Well? How do you feel? Scared?"

I was hoping he'd say yes, but of course he didn't. The iguana shook his head and stared out to sea. He must have forgotten about having to brave its waters and risk his life in the process. He was simply staring in awe, as if struck by the beauty and majesty of the ocean. I squatted down next to the iguana and looked at the waves crashing over the beach and the shimmering wet sand that changed color every few minutes. I might have been awestruck too by the beauty of the ocean if this were any other time, but right now I was anxious about what was to come. About the iguana that would surely drown in the hostile sea.

Was it too late to stop him?

This was the only thought I had obsessed over the last few days. What could I do to make the iguana stay? I knew it was no use to sob and cling to him. Should I dive into the ocean and insist on coming with him? Briefly, I'd considered locking him up in the house. But if the kindhearted iguana decided to stay because of me, what would that mean for him? When I thought of what I would be doing to him, I felt my throat close up and my chest turn heavy. I kept grabbing and releasing fistfuls of sand. A part of me wanted to cry like a child throwing a tantrum, and another part of me didn't want to say anything stupid to ruin this moment.

"Thank you for everything," the iguana said quietly. He sounded as if he knew what I was thinking. I opened my mouth to say something but nothing came out. I knew I would regret the words I would say no matter what they were.

Soon, the iguana crawled out to sea. He took easy, straight steps as if he were going for a short walk. At the point where the water met the beach, he took a big step forward without a moment's hesitation, then leaped. The waves rocked him side to side for a few moments, but soon the creature found his balance. He began swimming as he had been taught. Using his front and back legs, he took long, careful strokes, his head lifted above the surface, face forward.

I sat and watched until the iguana grew farther and farther away until he was a dot in the horizon, and disappeared altogether. Then I got up to go home.

I headed to the train station. After purchasing a ticket, I sat in an empty bench at the depot. I stared into the distance, fingering the empty aquarium I'd place in the seat next to me. Then I realized something. I hadn't given the iguana a name. We'd been together for so long and I'd truly wished him all the best and yet I hadn't even given him a name before sending him off to a place I'd never see him again.

With deep regret came the memories of that fateful afternoon and my ex-boyfriend's back when I'd asked what the name of the iguana was. The day seemed so long ago, almost a lifetime ago, although it wasn't. For some reason, the back that was turned towards me seemed to represent little pieces of all those who had turned away from me over the years. Dabbing at my eyes with my sleeve, I sat and sobbed softly until the train finally arrived.

After the monsoons came a late summer heat that soon gave way to fall.

The new hire at the pool quit her job in September without bothering to give her notice, claiming she had to go back to school. This meant I had to take on all the extra shifts until we could hire her replacement. I came home utterly exhausted. Still, I remembered to have a nice potted plant delivered to Eugene's studio in time before the opening. Eugene called me as soon as the plant arrived and thanked me in an eager, excited voice. She then asked if I was still working at the pool. I muttered something that wasn't exactly an answer, then hung up.

At night, I curled up into a ball and waited for sleep to come. My body was exhausted, but sleep remained elusive no matter how much I tossed and turned. It felt like I had a hopelessly tangled ball of string inside my head in place of a brain. Each time I turned over in bed, I let out a low moan. When I closed my eyes and opened them again, I saw that dawn had come without warning.

Until one day.

It was a day like any other day. I dragged myself home from work. Glancing at my mailbox, I saw something sticking out of a corner. I pulled at it, thinking it was likely an advert that I'd have to throw away, but the feel of the paper was softer and thicker than some cheap ad. Even before I'd taken it out to study it closely, I knew what I was holding in my hand. It was a postcard.

Unable to make a sound, I clutched at the postcard and brought it close to my eyes. It was a square postcard the size of my palm, with a photograph taking up one whole side. It appeared to be a photo taken of a dry plain, with sharp, jagged rocks scattered among bunches of low brush. Canary yellow flowers were bursting in full bloom near the trunks of a few trees, their leaves broad and thick. And there were iguanas. Iguanas everywhere. Iguanas on top of rocks, iguanas clinging to trees, iguanas hiding in the brush. They were all sunning themselves, each in a most comfortable position. They looked to be healthy and living their best lives, with not a worry or care in the world.

I turned the postcard over. The edges were decorated beautifully with flowers and leaves. On one side were a few printed lines, presumably for the sender to scribble a few notes in, but there was nothing written there. Instead, on the blank space next to the lines, was a blurred print of something. Only after I'd held it up to the light did I see it was a print of an iguana's foot.

So, he'd arrived safe.

Overjoyed, I looked up and noticed that snow was falling, as if by magic. It was heavy, significant snow, the kind that turned the whole world white. Holding the postcard in one hand, I stared at the snow. It wasn't snowing when I'd walked home a few minutes earlier. I had no way of knowing when the snowfall began.

I pushed open the doorway and stood outside in the snow. Snowflakes landed on my flushed cheeks and earlobes. From somewhere far away came the shrieks of excited children. I tilted my head back and looked up at the sky for a long time, then, as if I'd meant to all along, began going back the way I'd come, back to the swimming pool.

AUTHOR'S NOTE

A long time ago, I happened to come across a handsome clock. Looking for a place to hang it up, I finally discovered a nail sticking out of a wall in one of the smaller rooms of the house. It was the perfect place, so perfect that I wondered why I hadn't hung anything there before. It wasn't easy hanging the clock. The snowman-shaped hole in the back of the clock, meant for the nail, was much too small, and the nail itself was even smaller. Repeatedly, I tried turning the clock over to check where the hole was, then attempted to align the hole with the nail over and over again, but the nail and the hole never seemed to meet. I pressed the clock to the wall and stood there twisting and rubbing it against the wall, hoping to make contact with the nail. Then suddenly, the clock made an unexpected clicking sound as the hole finally found the nail (the hole was apparently much lower down the clock than I thought, near the center of the clock's body), and thereafter the clock looked as if it had always belonged on the wall, ever since the house was first built.

Stepping down from the chair where I'd been standing, I thought of how similar this was to writing a work of fiction and made a mental note to keep this moment locked up in my memory so that when the time came and I'd done better for myself than I'd thought and was about to publish my own book, I could tuck this little anecdote in as part of the author's note in the book's back pages. Which is what I'm doing now.

Fall 2021
Lee Yuri